Also by Hazel Holt

Mrs. Malory and the Festival Murder
Mrs. Malory and the Shortest Journey
Mrs. Malory: Detective in Residence
Mrs. Malory Wonders Why
Mrs. Malory: Death of a Dean
Mrs. Malory and the Only Good Lawyer
Mrs. Malory: Death Among Friends
Mrs. Malory and the Fatal Legacy
Mrs. Malory and the Lilies That Fester
Mrs. Malory and the Delay of Execution
Mrs. Malory and Death by Water
Mrs. Malory and Death in Practice
Mrs. Malory and the Silent Killer
Mrs. Malory and No Cure for Death
Mrs. Malory and a Death in the Family

MRS. MALORY AND A TIME TO DIE

A Sheila Malory Mystery

Hazel Holt

AN OBSIDIAN MYSTERY

OBSIDIAN
Published by New American Library, a division of
Penguin Group (USA) Inc., 375 Hudson Street,
New York, New York 10014, USA
Penguin Group (Canada), 90 Eglinton Avenue East, Suite 700, Toronto,
Ontario M4P 2Y3, Canada (a division of Pearson Penguin Canada Inc.)
Penguin Books Ltd., 80 Strand, London WC2R 0RL, England
Penguin Ireland, 25 St. Stephen's Green, Dublin 2,
Ireland (a division of Penguin Books Ltd.)
Penguin Group (Australia), 250 Camberwell Road, Camberwell, Victoria 3124,
Australia (a division of Pearson Australia Group Pty. Ltd.)
Penguin Books India Pvt. Ltd., 11 Community Center, Panchsheel Park,
New Delhi - 110 017, India
Penguin Group (NZ), 67 Apollo Drive, Rosedale, North Shore 0632,
New Zealand (a division of Pearson New Zealand Ltd.)
Penguin Books (South Africa) (Pty.) Ltd., 24 Sturdee Avenue,
Rosebank, Johannesburg 2196, South Africa

Penguin Books Ltd., Registered Offices:
80 Strand, London WC2R 0RL, England

First published by Obsidian, an imprint of New American Library,
a division of Penguin Group (USA) Inc.

First Printing, December 2008
10 9 8 7 6 5 4 3 2 1

PUBLISHER'S NOTE
This is a work of fiction. Names, characters, places, and incidents either are the
product of the author's imagination or are used fictitiously, and any resem-
blance to actual persons, living or dead, business establishments, events, or
locales is entirely coincidental.

The publisher does not have any control over and does not assume any
responsibility for author or third-party Web sites or their content.

For my granddaughter Natalie
With love and thanks for her help
with all the horsey bits

*To every thing there is a season, and a time to
every purpose under the heaven:
A time to be born, and a time to die.*

—Ecclesiastes 3:1

Chapter One

"Keep his head up, Fiona! Straighten up, Jemma. You're like a sack of potatoes! Poppy, don't check him too soon. That's good, Hannah. Keep him moving!"

I watched, with some affection, the tall woman taking a class of young riders in the ring.

"Jo really is fantastic," I said to my friend Rosemary. "She must be seventy if she's a day. She's so full of energy; she never stops! How does she do it?"

"Oh, metabolism," Rosemary said, "or whatever they call it. Some people have it and some people haven't. I haven't."

"Oh, nor do I, but I do envy people who have. I mean, just looking at all this"—I gestured towards the stables, the fields with horses grazing and the ring set up with jumps in the field below—"makes me long to go for a ride again. After all, I'm younger than Jo, but I just *know* how much I'd ache and how nervous I'd be about injuring myself. Feeble, isn't it?"

"Nonsense," Rosemary replied robustly, "just sensible. Jo's been riding every day of her life for the last goodness knows how many years. You haven't. Anyway," she continued with the candor of an old friend, "you've never been much of a one for taking exercise."

The voice from below went on. "Martha, keep your hands *down*. Don't pull at his mouth like that! Jemma, lower leg *forwards*!"

Clear and mellifluous, each word audible even at this distance, it was a splendid voice, as well it might be. Josephine Howard, as she was then, was used to making herself heard at the back of the upper circle without a microphone. We tend to forget that Jo was one of the leading actresses of her day. Looking at her now, with her brown, weatherbeaten face and untidy, cropped gray hair, it's difficult to trace the beauty that illuminated her Rosalind, her Viola and her enchanting Beatrice. Just occasionally a graceful movement or gesture brings back memories. And there's the voice, of course.

"I wonder," I said, "if she ever regrets giving it up—the stage, I mean."

"She seems happy enough," Rosemary said, "and she still adores *him*."

At the height of her career Jo had abandoned the theater to marry Charlie Hamilton, and embraced with enthusiasm his world of horses. It wasn't surprising, I suppose; his charm was legendary. In our cynical age, charm is something dubious, almost a pejorative term, but Charlie's was the real thing. It still is. He's one of the nicest people I know and the niceness has survived some pretty awful bad luck.

When he married Jo, he was a brilliant show jumper, Olympic standard. He bred his own horses and rode them magnificently. Until, that is, he had a bad fall and his leg never mended properly. He went on breeding horses, but the business didn't prosper. He was let down badly by some financial backers, and it was Jo who finally called a halt. She persuaded him to come back to Taviscombe, where she'd been born and brought up, and set up the riding school with their remaining capital. Through determination and hard work she'd made it a success, and the quieter life seems to suit them.

Just then we saw Charlie crossing the stable yard. He'd finally and reluctantly taken to a walking stick, which he raised in greeting when he saw us. We waved back, and Rosemary said, "You can see why she does—adore him, I mean."

We watched him fondly as he went into one of the horse boxes. He doesn't ride anymore but still gives the occasional lesson and is always busy with the horses in one way or another.

"When you think," Rosemary went on, "about the sort of life he's had and how unlucky he's been, it's amazing that he never seems bitter or resentful—always cheerful and in good spirits."

"And Jo's the same," I agreed. "I suppose they're content, and how many of us can say that?"

A small group of riders appeared in the distance.

"Oh, good," Rosemary said, "that's Delia's ride coming back. I hoped they'd be back on time because I've got to collect Alex from his piano lesson at half past."

Rosemary's daughter, Jilly (my goddaughter), has a sprained ankle and can't drive, so Rosemary has taken on the task of ferrying her grandchildren to and from the many social and leisure activities that the young seem to need to engage in nowadays.

"*We* were never driven about everywhere," I said. "We went by bus or on our bikes."

"Goodness, yes," Rosemary said, laughing. "Do you remember that time we cycled to the Valley of Rocks and you got a puncture? It started to get dark and our parents were frantic—no phones anywhere, of course, and certainly no mobiles!"

"But it was practically the only time they *did* get frantic," I said. "We had so much more freedom then. And, actually, Michael and your two got about quite a bit on their own."

"I think," Rosemary said thoughtfully, "that was just about the end of the age of innocence. Before all the dreadful tabloid stories and the horrors on television. And there was less traffic even then. I know Jilly gets really anxious when Alex insists on cycling to school." She sighed. "Sad, but I don't think we'll ever get back to the way things were."

The riders had now dismounted, and I saw Delia leading her horse back into the yard.

"Oh dear," Rosemary said, "I hope she's not going to hang around there. I do want to get back for Alex, and once she gets into those stables . . ."

But Delia emerged quite soon.

"Hello, Gran," she said, taking off all the impediments that safety regulations seem to require (I know they're sensible, but I'm always delighted to see the Queen out riding, wearing a head scarf).

Delia acknowledged my presence in the casual way the young do.

"Did you have a nice ride, darling?" Rosemary asked.

"Yes, I had Tsar. I love him; he's very lively."

"That gray one looks nice too," Rosemary said. "He looks just like the old rocking horse I had when I was a child."

Delia looked at her grandmother in horror. "Gran, how could you! Someone might have heard you—so embarrassing!"

She wrenched open the rear door of the car, flung her riding things inside and scrambled in after them, presumably in case any of her friends saw her with people who made such uncool remarks. Rosemary looked at me and pulled a face, and I smiled back.

However, in the car—presumably safe from the observation of her peers—Delia held forth at great length about the glories of the ride.

"We had a lovely lot of cantering. Tsar canters really well; he really likes to go. And we got as far as the Giant's Chair this time. You know how last time it was too windy high up there and the horses were getting spooked. Tsar tried to bolt, but I pulled him round all right. Liz said I did really well. Gran, do you think Daddy *will* see about that loan pony we saw advertised? If *you* speak to him,

I'm sure he will. Liz said there's room for us to keep him at livery here. Oh yes, and Mummy said I could have another jumping lesson, so I booked in for next Friday, and Charlie said he'd be taking it! Isn't that wicked!"

Not surprisingly, Charlie is something of a hero with the young who frequent the stables, and he's wonderful with them. He and Jo have no children of their own but are always surrounded with a crowd of the young. Mostly girls, of course.

When Rosemary dropped me off at home on her way to pick up Alex ("He's completely unmusical," Rosemary says, "but Jilly thinks piano lessons are somehow good for him—I can't imagine why!"), I let the animals out and, on an impulse, got out one of the old photograph albums that live in the chest in the hall. I turned over the pages and smiled at the pictures of my younger self, formally dressed in boots, breeches and hacking jacket with a shirt and tie, on Prudence, an elderly mare who once lost her head and bolted with me, trying to join the hunt when she heard the sound of the hounds in the distance. There were photographs of Michael in riding gear too, but boys seem to grow out of their horsey phase more quickly than girls, and he soon gave it up in favor of fishing and ferreting. I suppose it won't be long, though, before Alice wants to ride too.

My thoughts were interrupted by the phone. Its ring seemed to have a particularly imperious tone and I wasn't surprised to find that the caller was my friend Anthea. Brunswick Lodge is a large house, the center of most of the social activities of Taviscombe. It is staffed entirely by volunteers who, as is well-known, need a very firm hand to control them. Anthea is that firm hand.

"Where have you been?" she demanded, without any sort of preamble. "I've been trying to get you all afternoon."

"I went with Rosemary to fetch Delia from the riding stables," I said, an apologetic note creeping involuntarily into my voice.

"Oh." From Anthea's tone I gathered she didn't think it was much of an excuse. "Well, anyway, it's about the bring and buy next Wednesday morning. Can you take over? Maureen says she's got to go to visit her mother in hospital in Taunton, though why she can't go in the afternoon, I don't know."

At times like this one doesn't say no to Anthea, and I found myself agreeing to do far more than simply "take over"—providing cakes and scones, for example, and arranging for the trestle tables to be picked up from the Scouts' Hall. I was just about to ring off when Anthea suddenly said, "Oh yes, and talking about the stables, you know Charlie Hamilton, don't you?"

"Well, yes," I said warily.

"I thought it might be a good idea to get him to give a talk about show jumping and all that sort of thing when we start our autumn season. It might bring in some of the younger people. We could do with some young blood. The over-sixties are all very well, but we have to look to the future."

Since Anthea's views on the young are usually condemnatory to put it mildly, this was quite a turnaround. Still, I was determined to not get involved.

"Not really a good idea," I said. "I don't think it would be tactful to ask him to talk about the old days."

"Whyever not?" Anthea is not renowned for her tact.

"Oh, you know, the way everything fell apart for him, the memories must still be very painful."

"What nonsense." I sometimes wonder if Anthea has ruthlessly expunged from *her* memory anything that might give her the slightest feeling of disquiet. "Oh well," she went on, "I'll have a think about it and get back to you."

As it turned out, Ron Murphy, who usually fetches the trestles for us, was away on holiday. ("What he wants to go to *Egypt* for, I don't know," his sister said when I rang. "I blame all these television programs about pyramids and pharaohs and nonsense like that. *I* wouldn't cross the street to see one of those horrible mummy things—morbid, if you ask me!") As a result I had to try to make other arrangements, without success, so I had to fall back on my last hope—Michael.

"I know you're busy, darling," I said, "but it'll take you only half an hour and I'd be so grateful. There'll be someone there to help you load them into the Land Rover."

"I suppose I could manage Thursday evening,"

Michael said, "but in return, I've a favor to ask you."

"Of *course*. What is it?"

"Will you look after your granddaughter next Friday? Thea and I want to go to Taunton to see poor old Jonah. He's just had his gallbladder out and is feeling a bit low, and frankly, I don't think Alice and hospital visiting are a good mix."

"Very wise. Of course you must go and see Jonah—he's your best friend after all. Do give him my love. And I'd love to have Alice. If it's a nice day, we could go to the beach."

As it turned out we didn't go to the beach because Rosemary rang me that morning in some agitation.

"Sheila, I hate to ask, but could you possibly collect Delia from her riding lesson this afternoon? Jilly's out of action and Roger's taking Alex to the cricket, and now I've just heard from Mother that she's made an appointment to have her eyes tested. Mr. Mackenzie doesn't usually see people in the afternoon, but she persuaded him! And she didn't think to tell me until this morning. I can take Delia to the stables, but if you could collect her at three o'clock and take her back with you, I'll fetch her as soon as I've sorted Mother out."

Since Mrs. Dudley is another person one doesn't say no to, I quite understood Rosemary's predicament.

"No, that's fine. I'm looking after Alice, but I'm

sure she'd love to go to see the horses. Unless," I said, "you think Delia might find it *embarrassing*."

Rosemary laughed. "Apparently it doesn't work like that. Small children are all right—at least small *girls* are. They can be bossed about and patronized. She'll be delighted to have someone to show off to."

We got to the stables early and stood watching Delia in the ring below with two other girls. Charlie stood there, leaning on his stick and calling out instructions while Liz, one of the stable girls, moved forward occasionally to pick up a pole that had been knocked down. Alice was enthralled and tugged at my arm.

"Gran, Gran, can we go down and see them? I want to see the horses!"

"Hallo, Sheila." Jo had come up behind me. "And who have we here?"

"Oh, hello, Jo. This is my granddaughter, Alice."

"Hello, Alice. Would you like to come and see *my* horses?"

Alice, who is usually shy with strangers, took Jo's hand immediately, and they went off towards the stable yard. When I caught up with them, Jo had lifted Alice up to stroke the nose of a large chestnut whose head protruded from one of the loose boxes.

"It's all right," Jo said to me. "Captain's very gentle."

"Captain," Alice said with satisfaction, "*likes* me stroking him." And, as Jo put her down she asked, "Can I ride him?"

"He's too big for you," Jo said. She thought for a moment, and then she called out to the other stable girl, who was filling a hay net, "Pam, could you bring Cracker out into the yard, please."

Pam led a small Exmoor pony from one of the stables and put a saddle and bridle on him. Jo turned to me. "She'll be quite safe on him. Pam will hold him. Is that all right?"

Alice was wild with excitement, so I nodded.

Jo lifted her onto the pony's back and said, "Hold on tight to his mane."

"I want to hold the strings," Alice said, so Jo showed her how to hold the reins, and Pam slowly walked the pony round the yard.

Jo smiled. "A natural. Look how well she's sitting down. How old is she?"

"She's seven, nearly eight," I said.

"The perfect age to start," Jo said. "And no, I'm not touting for customers. I just think, like I said, that she's a natural, and she's obviously enjoying it."

"I'll have to see what Thea and Michael think," I said.

Pam brought Cracker back round the yard towards us. I was amused to see Alice's solemn face, concentrating hard on what she was doing.

"She did very well," Pam said, lifting her down. "She's full of confidence."

"Did you see me, Gran?" Alice was all excitement again. "Can I come ride Cracker again—ride him properly?"

"We'll have to see, darling," I said, but I knew

from experience that once Alice had set her mind on something, she was unstoppable.

We collected Delia, and all the way home and while they were both having tea, Delia and Alice talked horses. Or rather Delia laid down the law, and Alice, her fervent acolyte, drank it all in.

When Thea and Michael called to collect her, I explained what had happened (with antiphonal comments from Alice) and told them what Jo had said. With some relief I learned that Thea used to be a keen rider in her youth.

"I've been meaning to get back into it," she said, "but I never got around to it. I'd love to go with Alice."

"Jo's a very good teacher," Michael said, "and Charlie was wonderful. He could still go hacking when I was learning—that was before his leg got so bad—and it was a terrific experience to go out with him. No, if Jo says Alice is up to it, and if"—he turned to his daughter—"*if* she's a very good girl, then I don't see why we shouldn't give it a try."

"Oh well," Rosemary said when I told her about it, "it had to happen sooner or later. And, really, it's been marvelous this holiday. Delia spends all her time up at the stables—never wants to go anywhere else. Not just riding, but mucking out and cleaning tack, polishing bits and bridles and so forth."

"Most stables are partly run on child labor," I said.

"Very true," Rosemary agreed. "It was so funny,

the first time Delia asked Jo if she could help around the stables, Jo agreed and then gave her a bucket of water, some soap and a brush, and told her to scrub down all the tables and things in the tack room."

"Goodness!"

"And Delia was thrilled—Delia, who considers herself martyred if she has to stack the dishwasher, and as for tidying her room . . . !"

I smiled. "Little girls and horses," I said. "And I can see *I'm* going to be hanging around stables quite a bit myself from now on."

Chapter Two

"Are you going to Dunster Show?" Rosemary asked.

"I don't know; it depends on the weather," I replied. "It was pretty miserable last year, trailing about in the rain and absolutely *ghastly* trying to get the car out—all that mud. Lots of people had to be pulled out by tractors."

"The forecast isn't bad. Overcast but not actually wet. I said I'd go with Jilly and the children. Roger's working, of course. Delia's mad to see the horses. One of her school friends is showing her pony and she says Delia can help her groom it beforehand, so we'll have to get there early. Do come and we can lunch together in the Members' Tent."

"I might go with Michael and Thea, in the Land Rover so we don't get stuck. I expect Thea—and Alice now—will want to watch the jumping. I love watching for a bit, but they're always hours behind and it goes on forever, so lunch with you would be a marvelous excuse for getting away!"

We've all been going to the show ever since we were children, and every year for the last I don't know how long we've all said we're not going *this*

year—it's too exhausting, too crowded, and, anyway, not what it was—but, in the end, we usually
do go. It's not just the show itself that draws us,
but, really, it's a way of catching up with people
we hardly ever see at other times, old friends from
way back, people who've moved away, but who
come back "one more time," a chance to catch up
on the news.

"It's not only Jilly and the children," Rosemary
said, "but Mother expects me to go, now that she
can't manage to get there herself, to take back the
gossip."

"Oh well," I said, "there'll be plenty of that in
the Members' Tent. Drinking gin and tonics rather
too early in the day does seem to loosen tongues
quite remarkably."

The weather wasn't too bad—gray and chilly—
a typical English August day, in fact. We got there
quite early and wandered round, looking at the
livestock—the massive Red Devon cattle and jolly
little Dexters, and all the wonderfully woolly
Exmoor Horn sheep, the only breed I can recognize. After a bit we met up with Rosemary and her
family, who were sitting on straw bales round the
ring, waiting for the horsey events.

"Oh, poor Jilly," I said. "Is your wrist still in
plaster?"

"No, it's just bound up now and getting on quite
well, but I thought I'd put it in a sling so that, with
any luck, people won't jostle me."

"Where's Delia?" Alice demanded.

"She's helping her friend with a pony, but she'll

be back here soon," Rosemary said. She made a place for us beside her, and Michael took Alex, who was getting restive at the lack of activity, to look at the tractors and other assorted farm machinery. Delia joined us just as the tannoy was urging the child's pony novice class to "go into the collecting ring *now*."

"Rachel's awfully nervous," Delia said, addressing Alice as the only person present worthy of the information, "and Muffet—that's her horse, a Welsh mountain pony that is absolutely marvelous—was playing up. I had to hold him while she was plaiting his mane and tail, but he settled down, so I think she'll be all right."

A series of girls rode around the ring, each one criticized sharply by Delia, until Rachel came in on her neat little pony. She walked, trotted and cantered, and then joined the others waiting hopefully to be called up by the judges.

"Oh look," Delia burst out excitedly, "they're calling her up! Oh, wonderful Muffet, he's standing *beautifully*! She's got a third; isn't that brilliant!"

We all clapped enthusiastically as the three winners did their lap of honor, clutching their rosettes. Delia promptly disappeared, presumably to congratulate her friend, and the rest of us settled down to watch the next event.

"It's the hunter mare up to fifteen hands," Thea said, consulting her program, "with own foal at foot. I love this one; the foals are so enchanting! Oh look, isn't that Jo with the chestnut and that lovely little foal? I didn't know they were still breeding horses."

"Just one or two, but not to sell on," I said. "Jo couldn't bear to give up altogether."

We watched Jo's slim figure, elegant in the black jacket and formal gear, so unlike her usual everyday self, and we applauded vigorously when she won her class.

When that was over Rosemary got to her feet. "I must go and walk about a bit. I'm getting stiff. Straw bales weren't meant for the over-sixties. Are you coming, Sheila?"

I looked at Thea inquiringly.

"You go," she said. "I'd rather like to see the jumping, and I'm sure Alice would too. We'll see you for lunch."

Rosemary looked at her watch as we moved away. "Just time for a quick prowl round the stalls; then we'll go for a drink."

I fell victim to a rather nice leather handbag and a new Barbour waterproof hat. Rosemary bought a tweed waistcoat for herself and a cap for Jack ("I always have to take him back a fairing," she said, "though he doesn't deserve it because he never comes himself"), and we made our way through the crowds to the Members' Tent. Although it was still early, the place was quite full. I found a table while Rosemary got the drinks.

"Nice to sit in a proper chair," Rosemary said as she poured the tonic into her glass, "even if it is a bit wobbly. And thank goodness they still have real glasses in here and not those awful plastic things. Now then, who's here?"

Greetings were exchanged with various people and news was shouted across from other tables, against the background roar of conversation.

"Have you ever noticed," I said, "how the canvas walls of the tent seem to magnify the noise? I suppose they act as a sort of sounding board."

"I know. I really couldn't hear properly what Dick Fraser was telling me. Did he really say that Elaine has gone off to Inverness with *Malcolm Hartman*?"

"I think so, though I must say it does seem unlikely! Oh look, there's Charlie. Do wave to him to come and sit here."

Charlie Hamilton, looking rather worn and leaning heavily on his stick, made his way towards us.

"Great heavens, what a crush!" he said as he sat down gratefully. "I always forget how crowded everywhere is."

"I'll get some drinks," I said. "Whiskey for you, Charlie?"

When I got back, Rosemary was saying how glad we were that Jo had won her class, and how splendid she looked.

Charlie smiled. "The old girl still turns out pretty well," he said, "and we're very pleased with Starlight. She's come on beautifully, and that's a really nice little foal she dropped."

"I'm so glad you haven't given up breeding altogether," I said.

"Well, it creates a bit more interest for Jo," Charlie said, "and I like to see the young ones about." He turned to Rosemary. "Your Delia's coming along well."

"She's mad keen," Rosemary said, "and, of course, she's longing for her own pony. I expect she'll wear Jilly and Roger down. I don't know how much longer they'll be able to hold out!"

"I think I might know of a loan pony," Charlie said. "I'll make some inquiries. . . ."

He broke off as he spotted two people coming in. "Oh, there's Esther and Simon. Is there room for them to join us?"

Esther Nicholson is Jo's sister, but totally unlike her in every way. Where Jo is tall and elegant, Esther is short and plump; where Jo is cool and witty, Esther is fidgety and never stops talking. Jo went away and made a brilliant career for herself; Esther stayed at home and, after a brief spell as a receptionist, married Gordon Nicholson, the dentist she worked for. Simon is their son, and more like his aunt (whom he's devoted to) than either of his parents. He's an accountant and looks after the books at the stables.

"Hello," Rosemary said. "Lovely to see you. Pull up a couple of chairs, Simon. There's plenty of room here."

"Well," Esther said, flopping down into a chair and arranging a collection of plastic bags round her feet, "I've never known it so crowded. You can hardly get into some of the trade tents. I'm sure the girl in the produce tent didn't pack that honeycomb properly; she was so busy." She bent down and rummaged in one of the bags. "No, it seems to be all right, but it's in the bag with the smoked-trout pâté and the wild-boar sausages, and you wouldn't want honey all over *those*, now would you? Simon, I'll have a gin and tonic if you can get to the bar."

"How about everyone else?" Simon asked.

Rosemary and I shook our heads, and Charlie said, "I'll wait till lunch, thanks all the same."

"It gets worse every year," Esther went on. "I don't think I'll come again. It's not what it was—not like the old days. It's getting too commercial—and not a proper band, just taped music and all those motor bikes doing acrobatics or whatever it is they do. Anyway, it's nice to see you both. How have you been keeping? I saw Jilly just now, Rosemary. She had her arm in a sling. Has she broken it? And I didn't expect to see Michael here, Sheila. I thought lawyers never took a day off—too busy making money!" She laughed. "Did you see Jo and that horse of hers? She really is getting too old for all that, Charlie. I don't know why you let her do it."

Knowing Esther of old, none of us felt it necessary to answer what were obviously rhetorical questions. Fortunately, Simon came back with the drinks, so she was obliged to stop talking while she drank her gin and tonic.

"Well, *you've* taken a day off," Rosemary said to Simon, smiling. Simon used to work for Jack's firm of accountants when he first started out and

Rosemary has always had a soft spot for him. We both feel sorry for him having to cope with Esther. Gordon has more or less given up and, at home at least, has gone into a kind of monosyllabic retreat, giving all his energies to outside activities like the Rotarians and the local council.

"I usually take a week of my leave around now," he said. "I'm going to spend a few days in London."

"Theaters and galleries?" I asked.

"This and that," Simon said. "I haven't decided yet."

"Oh, Simon's not a one for museums and all that," Esther broke in. "We used to take him to all sorts of things when he was little. Do you remember, Simon, when we used to stay with Aunt Mavis?" She turned to me. "She's Gordon's older sister, married a consultant—orthopedics, always pays well!—and they have a house in Richmond, huge great place; must be worth a fortune now. No," she went on, "Simon never took any interest in that kind of thing. Vicky, now, she loved it all, but then she's always been the clever one." Vicky is Simon's sister and their mother's favorite. "She got a first, you know, at Oxford—such a pity she never did anything *with* it, going into the BBC like that."

"But she's done awfully well," Rosemary said. "She's a producer now, isn't she?"

"Yes," Esther said, "but only *radio*."

Vicky is very ambitious and simply couldn't wait to go away to London, without the slightest qualm about leaving Simon to bear the brunt of things at home. I do feel sorry for him. He's so good with both his parents and doesn't really have much of a life—just work and home and doing things around the stables. I know he likes being there with Jo and Charlie, so I suppose that's something. He did have a nice girlfriend, Julie Phillips, the daughter of one of the partners of his firm, but her job took her away to London and long-distance relationships never seem to work. That was more than a year ago and, as far as I know, he hasn't found anyone since. I did wonder, though, when he said he was going to London, whether he was going to see her.

Jo came in then and we all congratulated her on her first prize.

"Yes, I'm really pleased with Starlight," she said. "I think she's going to be something special. Freddy Barnet—he's one of the judges—he said that she's really first class. You know him, Charlie; we met him at the Bath and West last year. Oh, thank you, Simon." She turned and smiled at him as he handed her a drink. "Just what I needed! Liz is seeing to Starlight—we have to stay on for the President's Cup—but I must go and take over when I've had some lunch. I couldn't eat anything first thing—too nervous."

"Like a first night?" Rosemary suggested.

"Oh, worse, though that was always bad enough. But even for quite a small show it's worse because it's the horse as well, not just you."

The mention of lunch reminded me that I had to go and find my family, so I got up.

"I'd better come too," Rosemary said, "and drag Jilly and the children away from those horses and get some food into them!"

After lunch I wandered around for a bit, but quite soon I began to feel tired and was glad when Thea said, "I think Alice has had enough. Do you feel like coming away now?"

When I got home and had fed the animals (if I've been out all day their reproach takes the form of constant and repeated demands for food), I went upstairs to look for my old tweed hacking jacket, which I had promised to give to Thea now that she'd started riding again. It was many years since I'd worn it and I finally ran it to earth at the back of the cupboard in the spare room. It really is amazing the things one comes across if you're a hoarder like me. I found garments I'd had before Michael was born. Needless to say I couldn't get into any of them. I left them in a pile on the bed so that I'd be obliged to pack them all up for the charity shop. I suppose they're fashionable again by now—retro, I think the term is.

I tried on the hacking jacket and found that, amazingly, it still fitted me, and for one mad moment I thought perhaps I might start riding again, but common sense prevailed and I decided I really must have it cleaned before handing it on to Thea. I noted with resignation that Foss had curled up and was resolutely asleep among the clothes on the bed, and went downstairs to make myself a cup of tea.

A few days later I took the newly cleaned jacket round to Thea and asked her how she'd been getting on at the stables.

"The first few times were agony afterwards," she said. "All those muscles I haven't used for years! But it's fine now. Except that everything I learned now seems to be out of date."

"How could it be?" I asked.

"You know how it was *so* important to use your knees to control your horse? Well, it isn't now."

"Good heavens!"

"No, now it seems you have to use the whole of your lower leg. Well, you can imagine how difficult *that* is. I mean, all your instincts are to do things the way you always have."

"How awful."

"I think I'm getting the hang of it now. I've been out a couple of times with Liz, who tactfully reminded me, and once with Jo, who yelled at me when I forgot!"

I laughed. "At least Alice will be learning properly from scratch. Has she had any lessons yet?"

"Yes, a couple. On a leading rein, of course, though Jo, who's taking a real interest in her, thinks it won't be long before she can go on her own in the ring. Oh, I must show you something." She went away and came back with some very small jodhpurs and a pair of boots. "There! Aren't they gorgeous! I know it was silly of me, but she's so keen and was longing for the proper gear. Michael says I'm mad and we ought to wait and see how she gets on, but I was in that shop in Porlock where they have all the riding stuff and I couldn't resist!"

"Well," I said, "we won't have to worry now about what to give her for birthdays and Christmas."

"As long as it's not her own pony. Though I've no doubt Jo will have thoughts about that too!"

"How was Jo; is she all right? I thought she looked really tired at the show. I know she'd just been showing her horse and all that, but, just for a moment she really looked her age."

"No, she seemed all right when I saw her. She was a bit—well, I don't know quite what—not put out exactly, but disconcerted, I suppose. She'd heard from Vicky, who's making a radio program and wants to tape an interview with her."

"And?"

"I gather it's to be about the theater—past actors and so forth. Well, you know how Jo never likes talking about all that."

"No, I sometimes think she regrets her time as an actress and doesn't want to reminded about it. I remember Anthea once asked her to give a talk about her life in the theater at Brunswick Lodge and Jo was really quite rude to her. Anthea was absolutely amazed, because you know how amiable Jo always is. But she shut Anthea up, and that takes a lot of doing!"

"Oh well, perhaps she'll put Vicky off."

"I don't know about that. From what I remember, Vicky can be just as persistent as Anthea, and she does have the advantage of being Jo's niece. It will be interesting to see if she can pull it off."

Chapter Three

"Do you feel like coming with me to collect some chickens?" Thea asked me when she rang.

"Chickens?"

"Yes, I've always wanted to keep them, ever since I was a child, so, when I saw an advert for a chicken house in the *Free Press*, I thought why not!"

"Well, good for you. What does Michael think about it?"

"Since he knows *he* won't have to do anything about the actual hens, he's all for it. Anyway, he's installed the chicken house and put up a wire-netting pen, so I'm all set. I'm starting off with twelve to see how it goes."

"Splendid. Yes, I'd love to come. When?"

"Alice is spending the day with her friend Jessica tomorrow. Jessica's mother, bless her, is taking them both swimming and then back to lunch, so I thought that would be a good time to go. Could you come about ten thirty? I'm afraid we'll have to go in the Land Rover, so I pray this place isn't up a dreadfully narrow lane, because I'm hopeless at backing up in it!"

There was a narrow lane, leading up to the

rather scruffy-looking farmhouse high up, out over the moor, but fortunately no one else seemed to be using it that particular morning. A young woman, followed by a little girl, came out as we drove into the yard.

"You for the chicken, then?" she asked. "Dave left them all ready."

We followed her to a corner of the yard where there were two crates, each containing six rust-colored fowl, who clucked hysterically when the woman picked them up and swung them into the back of the Land Rover.

"Are they all right?" Thea asked anxiously.

"They'll soon settle down; don't you fret. If you can bring the crates back . . ."

The child, who had watched the whole proceedings with her finger in her mouth, took it out and pointed in the direction of the agitated birds.

"Chicken!" she said. "Chicken cross!"

Then, apparently overcome by her own temerity, she retreated behind her mother.

"We'll bring the crates back at the weekend if that's all right," Thea said. She handed over some money to the young woman, and we got back into the Land Rover and drove away.

After a little while I said, "I can't hear any noise from the chickens. Do you think they're all right?"

"I think so. Apparently they can't stand up while I'm driving, so they sit down and presumably await their fate with a sort of Asian stoicism. They'll be fine when we get them home."

And, indeed, they were. After a brief inspection

of the pen they pecked happily away at the corn Thea gave them and went into the chicken house as easily as if they'd always lived there.

"Well, that was good," I said. "I was afraid they might be temperamental."

"Oh, these are Warrens," Thea said, "not high-class, fancy birds—what Michael calls industrial grade—but uncomplicated and very good layers."

"That's all right, then. Are they going to be safe in there? I mean, what about foxes?"

"There's a sort of electric fence." She indicated the strands of wire going round the pen that she'd had to step over when she was seeing to them.

"Goodness," I said, "is it dangerous?"

"No, it's fine." She stooped to switch something on. "It gives quite a mild shock, enough to stop a fox or anything like that, but not too bad for humans. It runs off a battery. It's the big ones, you know, like the ones round fields, which run off the mains, that you have to be careful of. Anyway, they seem all right. I'll let them settle down for a bit and come back and look at them later. Let's go and have a cup of tea. I'm absolutely dying for one."

As I drove back home I thought about the way the wheel had come full circle, and how Thea had chosen to give up a successful career in the law to stay at home and cultivate the domestic virtues. I suppose it's a matter of temperament, and for some people it's perfectly possible to get complete satisfaction from that sort of life, while it would drive others mad. The trouble is, it seems to me, that, given the financial pressures of modern society, not many women *have* the option of choosing. In a way I didn't actually have a choice. My mother was an invalid for some years before she died, so I stayed at home to look after her, and after Michael too when he was young. But I was lucky; I had quite a bit of freelance work—writing books, articles, reviews and so forth—so I had the best of both worlds. And now I was finding that being a grandmother was both pleasurable and demanding.

The next day I decided that being able to do what I like when I like is very useful. My cousin (well, second cousin, really) Fred Prior telephoned to say he was back in England for a few days and asked if I would have lunch with him tomorrow. All Fred's arrangements tend to be ad hoc. He's some years older than I am, and more my parents' friend than mine. We hadn't seen each other for many years until he came back into my life quite recently. He's amazing for his age, full of energy and fun, with a wicked sense of humor, and we get on famously. He and his much-younger second wife now live in the south of France but, when he comes back to Bristol for business reasons, he always rings me and we have a splendid lunch together.

Nowadays I tend to avoid motorways, so on this occasion I decided to go to Bristol by train. As usual I arrived early for the train. Michael always used to say that if he counted up all the hours he'd spent waiting with me on railway platforms, he could have *written War and Peace*, let alone read it. There was only one other person on the platform when I arrived, a tall figure, instantly recognizable.

"Hello, Jo," I said. "Fancy seeing you here."

She turned quickly and seemed surprised and somehow disconcerted at being addressed, but then she said, "Sheila! Do forgive me; I was miles away!"

"Are you going to Bristol too?"

"Yes, I've got some tiresome business to see to. How about you?"

"Oh, lunch with my cousin—Fred Prior. Do you remember him?"

"Vaguely from down here. I used to see more of his first wife, Amanda, when she got married to Vernon Russell, the producer. They used to have rather grand parties at their house in Hampstead. And there was a son, wasn't there? He went into the profession, I seem to remember. He was a Charlie too—that's right, Charlie Prior."

"Actually, he gave up the stage, or acting, at least, and now he's a very successful agent."

"Good for him. That's a sensible move. There are too many actors! And what about Fred? He married again too, didn't he?"

"Yes, someone much younger, called Louise. She's half French, and they live in Antibes now. Fred's given up the Bristol house, but he comes over occasionally to see to things."

"I couldn't do that," Jo declared. "I couldn't live anywhere but England."

"Oh, nor could I. Abroad's all very well for holidays, but not for *living*, and, really, I don't think I'd want to live anywhere but Taviscombe—not just for the people, friends and family, but it's the only place where I really feel comfortable, if you know what I mean."

"Absolutely. That's why I came back here after—after we decided to set up the stables. It was a really bad time for us both. I just wanted to come home, I suppose."

I looked at Jo curiously. I'd never heard her mention that part of her life; all I knew had come from Simon, and Esther, of course. I was flattered, somehow, that she'd actually felt easy enough with me to mention it.

"I know what you mean," I said, feeling the urge to repay confidence with confidence. "When Mother died, and Peter, I wouldn't have been able to bear it anywhere else—not just the support from friends, but, well, it's something about your own *place*, somewhere you feel you belong."

Jo gave me one of her rare smiles. "Exactly," she said.

When the train came in, our reserved seats were in different carriages, so I didn't see her get off at Temple Mead station. But when Fred, who had come to meet me, and I were walking past the taxi rank, she was standing there, and I pointed her out to him.

"Yes, still the same old Jo Howard," he said. "She's worn well. I'd recognize her anywhere. But the poor old girl doesn't seem very happy—looks as if she's got the troubles of the world on her shoulders!"

Indeed, she did look drawn and anxious, and I wondered what sort of tiresome business it was that had brought her to Bristol.

The next time I saw her, though, I was glad to see that she was her old self again. I'd gone with Thea to watch Alice have a riding lesson at the stables and Jo was taking a class of older girls over the jumps, her voice ringing out cheerfully as she encouraged them.

"Here comes Cracker," Thea said as Liz led out the small Exmoor pony. Alice hesitated for a moment and then went resolutely towards them. She went to the mounting block and when she got onto the pony herself without any help, she turned and gave us a triumphant smile.

"She's still on a leading rein, of course," Thea said, "but she can rise to the trot now—there, look!"

Smiling indulgently, we watched her for a while, and then I said, "You stay here and I'll go and pay Peggy for her lesson."

I made my way through the stable block, past the tack room and into the office, though "office" is a rather grand name for the ramshackle wooden structure built onto one side of the tack room. Peggy wasn't there, but Charlie was, seated at a makeshift desk, making heavy weather of some forms. He looked up as I came in.

"Hello, Sheila. How are you with all this lot?"

He waved an official-looking booklet in the air. "Honestly, what with insurance, health and safety and God knows what else, I might as well be a bloody civil servant!"

"Oh don't!" I said. "I'm hopeless. I dash at them without reading them properly and then I find I've filled them in all wrong and they end up with masses of crossings out. Fortunately, Michael can't bear to see the mess I make of them, so he takes them away and sorts them for me."

Charlie smiled. "To be fair," he said, "Simon deals with most of our stuff, but he's still away and these have to go off before he gets back. He's a good lad; I don't know what we'd do without him, and he'll never take a penny for all the work he does for us."

"Oh well," I said. "Family."

Charlie sighed. "It's just as well," he said. "I don't know that we could afford to pay an accountant. Running a stable's an expensive business. That's why we've tried to expand the livery side. Weekenders and people like that will pay a fair amount for their riding, but then *that* means you've got to spruce things up a bit, make them feel they're getting value for money, and getting it all costs. Have you seen the price of hay now?"

I had to admit I hadn't.

"Criminal!" he said. "We've got a fair bit of pasture here, of course, but, even with that, the feed bills are terrible. And there's labor, of course. Liz and Peggy are marvelous workers and Jo slaves away every hour that God sends, and even I try to do my bit, but it's a struggle!"

"Well," I said, putting a couple of notes down on the desk, "here's a tiny bit towards it—the money for Alice's lesson."

He laughed. "Sorry, Sheila. I didn't mean to go on like that. You caught me at the wrong time; I'm not usually so dismal!"

"Oh, don't apologize. I know it does help sometimes to get things off your chest."

"I don't mind so much for myself," Charlie said. "I'd be quite happy with a few horses and a couple of regulars, but Jo cares so much about it. Anyway, thanks for this." He picked up the money, stood up, unlocked a small safe and put the notes into a cash box. "Every little bit helps!"

"You seem to have quite a few youngsters now," I said. "I imagine they'll be regulars for a while yet."

"Some of them will," Charlie said with a smile, "but some of them will discover boys and that will be the end of it."

"Oh well," I said, "you'll have Alice for a good many years. She's absolutely obsessed!"

"Jo says she's coming along very nicely." He broke off as there was a sudden noise and the sound of hooves clattering against wood. He limped out into the stable and I followed. Peggy was trying to calm down a large chestnut hunter that kept rearing up.

"Shorten the rein," Charlie said, "and bring his

head round. That's it. Good girl. Now he'll go into his stall. Take it gently."

He followed them and went over to the horse, stroking it and talking to it quietly. After a while he had a few words with Peggy and went out into the yard.

"That was Tarquin," he said to me, "just come in for livery and hasn't settled down properly yet. He's a bit temperamental and right now he's got a touch of laminitis, and that always makes them jumpy."

"Does he belong to a weekender?" I asked.

"As a matter of fact, no. He belongs to one of Gordon's council friends, Dan Webster. He's quite experienced; used to hunt with the D&S. But he's not a very good judge of horses; he goes for the showily good-looking ones. I think Tarquin's going to be a bit too much for him to handle, even when we've sorted out the laminitis."

"He's a very handsome creature," I said. "I can see how he might appeal."

"Oh well, we'll just have to do the best we can."

I stood in the doorway and looked out beyond the yard at the ring with the young riders and their ponies, then farther down, across the fields where some of the horses were grazing peacefully in the afternoon sunlight, towards the woods and in the distance to the hills, which were just beginning to turn purple and gold with the heather and gorse.

"It really is a glorious spot," I said to Charlie.

"I know," he said quietly. "We're very lucky.

Whatever happens, we have to keep hold of it somehow."

I went back to tea with Thea and Alice and, when Alice had finally exhausted every aspect of her ride ("And did you see me, Gran? I dismounted all by myself. I took both my feet out of the stirrups, like Liz said—you have to take them *right* out, and then you can get down. . . ."), I told Thea I thought Jo and Charlie might be having financial difficulties.

"It may just have been general grumbling," I said. "I mean, we all like to have a bit of a moan, but I have the feeling it was more than that and they're really worried."

"I thought riding stables simply coined money," Thea said. "They certainly charge enough!"

"Well, the expenses are high and it's all labor-intensive."

"But think of all that child labor—all those young girls who hang around, longing to be allowed to *do* something for the horses, however menial."

I thought of Delia scrubbing down the shelves and laughed. "Yes, there is that, but there's the feed and the equipment—saddles are a horrendous price, so Rosemary tells me. Apparently Roger is quite happy to look for a pony for Delia, and Jilly, who's not at all keen, keeps producing advertisements from Delia's horsey magazines to prove how hideously expensive everything is. And then, of course, they grow out of things so quickly—ponies as well as riding boots!"

"True."

"Anyway, Charlie seemed really worried. I've never seen him so down; you know how cheerful he usually is. And, come to think of it, when I saw Jo that time I went to Bristol, she looked very anxious about something and she did say she was there on business. Perhaps that was something to do with the stables."

"Trying to raise a loan do you think? Surely it can't be as bad as that. I mean, they own the land, don't they?"

"Oh yes. Well, I've never heard anything about it from either of them, but I'm sure Esther told me they used what money was left when Charlie had to sell up, to buy the whole setup, all those years ago, which I'm sure included the land. But they'd hate to have to sell a single field—well, I'm sure Jo would. Though I think, from what he said, Charlie would be perfectly happy to carry on in quite a small way."

"Jo's a perfectionist," Thea said. "She loves whatever she does and has to be the best—no half measures for her!"

"I know. I often wonder if that's part of the reason she gave up the stage. I mean, she'd done all the great classic roles and, after a certain age, there aren't that many parts for a woman. I don't think she could have borne to—well, come down from those heights."

Thea considered this for a moment and said, "You may be right. I don't suppose we'll ever know. Jo's never been one for talking about herself."

"No. Come to think of it, all we know about her life since she left Taviscombe we've heard from Esther, and Jo would never tell her anything really personal like that!"

Alice, who had just come back into the room, said, "When I have *my* pony, it can go and live at the stables with Cracker, can't it, Mummy?"

"Oh dear," I said to Thea, "it's started already. How long will you be able to hold out!"

Chapter Four

Every year I mean to buy my spring bulbs nice and early, but, what with one thing and another, I never seem to get around to it. When I finally do, there's practically nothing left except the rather forlorn piles of peeling daffodils, scruffy hyacinths and dried-up crocuses that have been picked over and discarded by other shoppers. Since I had a free afternoon for once, I went straight round to the garden center while the whole bulb situation was still uppermost on my mind.

Confronted by tempting boxes of newly arrived stock, I quite lost my head, filling the brown paper bags provided with practically every variety and every color on offer. I was just trying to decide between the merits of dwarf and parrot tulips when a voice behind me said, "You're going to be busy with that lot!"

Rapidly brought down to earth, I turned to answer Esther Nicholson. "Yes, I know," I said lightly. "I do seem to have gone a bit mad."

"But," she went on, "I don't suppose you still do your own gardening—it's not so easy when you get to our age."

"As a matter of fact," I said, annoyed at being classed with Esther, who is at least five years older than I am, if not more, "I do *all* the garden. Well," I added with a nod towards the truth, "except the heavy digging, of course. Reg Carter does that for me."

"Oh, do you find him satisfactory? We used to have him, but he wasn't very reliable."

"I've always found him absolutely fine," I said, conveniently forgetting the times I'd been maddened by his erratic timekeeping. I do find that conversation with Esther tends to bring out the worst in me. "Anyway," I went on, "how are you and Gordon?" I put my wire basket with the bulbs in it down on the floor, knowing from past experience that Esther always answers such trivial questions very fully.

"Oh, Gordon's been very busy. A lot of council stuff, you know, and then there's the Rotarians, of course. He's president this year and he's having to organize the trip to Belgium."

"How nice. Are you going?"

"I suppose I shall have to. I wouldn't have bothered if he hadn't been president, but you know how it is; it's expected of you. We've got to go through the Channel Tunnel and I can't say I fancy that—I mean, all that way under the sea! And Brussels, that's not very exciting. One of the trips is round the European Union buildings—not what you'd go abroad for, is it?"

"There's all that lovely Belgian chocolate," I suggested.

"Not with Gordon's heart and his cholesterol level, there isn't. No, I really don't feel like going anywhere just now."

"Really?"

"Between ourselves, I'm worried about Simon. He's working too hard, brings stuff home, up till all hours with that computer of his. I've seen the light on in his room at two o'clock, or three, even. I told him, you'll wear yourself out; you've got to get your proper rest. But of course he never listens; says he's fine. But he's looking really washed-out."

"But he's just been on holiday, surely . . ."

Esther gave a short laugh. "Much good it did him. He looked even worse when he got back. I said to him I don't know what you've been doing up in London, my lad, but it's certainly done you no good at all! But all he said was he had some late nights seeing friends." She sighed. "All those BBC types, friends of Vicky's, I suppose. He was staying with her. I hoped she might have talked some sense into him, but she's just the same; no idea of looking after herself. I'll be glad to have her down with me for a week—give her regular meals, not all these ready meals and takeaways that they seem to live on. Indian and Chinese—well, I tried Indian food once; you couldn't taste anything, it was so hot! As for Chinese—well, goodness knows what's in *that*! And now they all seem to be eating Japanese stuff, raw fish, if you can believe it! You can't tell me that's natural, or healthy either."

"Well," I said, hoping to stem the culinary tide,

"you'll be able to give her some lovely home-cooked food when she comes to stay."

"Roast lamb—she's always liked my roast lamb, and of course it's local, so we know where it *comes* from, and a nice cabbage from the garden and one of my apple tarts—the Bramleys will be just about ready by then."

"I'm sure she'll love that," I said, shifting my weight from one foot to the other and trying to look interested.

"Mind you," Esther went on, "I'm not prejudiced. When we go to France or Italy I always like the food there—well, almost all, some of it's a bit rich—but we've had some very nice meals in Paris and Florence. I always avoid the veal, of course—those poor little calves—but that's more Germany and Austria, isn't it? Escalopes and so forth."

"Yes, well . . . ," I said, tentatively trying to make a move.

"But"—Esther leaned towards me as if to increase the confidential nature of what she had to say—"the person I'm most worried about is Jo."

"Really?"

"She's not herself at all. She's getting very vague; hardly seems to take in anything I say to her. It looks as if her mind's elsewhere half the time. And she doesn't remember half the things I've been telling her about. I told her about our trip to Brussels only last week, but when I mentioned it yesterday she obviously hadn't taken in anything I'd said! I'm beginning to wonder if she's going into Alzheimer's. She's quite a bit older than I, you know."

"Surely not! She always seems so full of life and so much on the ball!"

Esther shook her head. "I think Charlie's worried about her too, though he denied there was anything wrong when I asked him."

"I'm sure everything's all right," I said reassuringly.

"Well, we'll see. Goodness, is that the time? I mustn't stand here chatting to you like this!" Having neatly put me in the wrong, she swept off to the checkout, where she caused a considerable holdup by having to go back to the shelves to hunt for a certain type of insecticide, which, it turned out, had been banned by the EU some months ago.

When I got home I put the bulbs carefully away in the larder (you're supposed to keep them cool) until I could empty the planters. I'd just put the kettle on when there was a ring at the door; it was Rosemary.

"Sorry to descend on you like this," she said, "but I was on my way back from Porlock and I thought I'd just pop in to see if you feel like coming out for lunch one day this week. It's been a really tiresome couple of days and I feel the need for a little treat."

"Oh dear, what's happened?"

"Well, it's Mother mostly—when is it not! She's been in one of her redecorating moods."

"Not painting and wallpapering!"

"No, not quite as bad as that, but curtains and covers. She says she can't *bear* to live with the present ones any longer."

"But she had those only eighteen months ago. I distinctly remember your having to go to Exeter to get some fabric she'd seen in a magazine."

"Don't remind me! No, this time it's something that chum of hers, Mrs. Watson, saw in a shop in Taunton. So I had to go and get a sample for her to see—several samples actually, because Mrs. Watson's description was so vague it could have been any one of half a dozen."

"And?"

"And, of course, none of them were right for her and, of *course*, it was my fault for being so stupid and not finding the right one. Honestly, Sheila, I almost *said* something, but what's the use? It's water off a duck's back with Mother!"

"Here," I said, passing her a cup of tea and pushing a plate of chocolate wafers towards her, "comfort food! So what happened?"

"Oh, she thought she might like that William Morris willow pattern fabric, so I dashed out and ordered some and phoned little Martha Cronin to come and measure up, all very quickly before she could change her mind."

"She might still change it."

"No, not now—money has been spent!"

"Poor you! And, yes, I'd love to come out to lunch. Would Thursday be all right? We might go to that new place in Lynton. They say it's very good and it's a nice little run to get there."

Rosemary leaned back in her chair and bit into a biscuit. "I mustn't stay too long; I've got to go and pick up Delia from the stables. She wants to get in as many rides as she can before school starts again and the nights start drawing in."

"I know—it's frightening how quickly the days get shorter. I always feel that after July it's downhill all the way to winter! Is Delia having a ride or a lesson?"

"Oh, a lesson. She's mad about jumping just now and Jo is a wonderful teacher."

"How do you think Jo is these days?" I asked.

"She seems fine. Why do you ask?"

"When I saw her last she looked a bit drawn and pale, and I've just had a dismal conversation about her with Esther."

I told her what Esther had said and Rosemary laughed. "I should think Jo *hadn't* been listening to Esther going on about Brussels! I mean, the only thing to do when Esther gets going is to think about something else until she stops. And, anyway, you know what she's like about saying how worried she is about everyone!"

"Well, she was certainly going on about Simon and Vicky as well."

"Oh, poor Simon—that boy is a saint. Anyone else would have moved out ages ago, but I think he feels it's only his being at home that keeps that family on some sort of even keel. So, what's the worry this time?"

"Oh, bringing work home, up till all hours at his computer—that sort of thing."

"Actually," Rosemary said thoughtfully, "I'm not really surprised—about bringing work home, I mean. Simon's good at his job, very thorough and reliable—Jack said he could trust him to cope with anything—but, because he's so thorough, he is a bit slow. The way things are nowadays, with everyone expecting things to be done absolutely at once, he may very well feel he's getting behind and needs to catch up at home."

"It really is dreadful," I said, "the way there's no *time* to do things properly. Not just business but doctors, even, having only ten minutes to give to each patient—though, thank goodness Dr. Macdonald belongs to the old school and jolly well gives it as long as it takes!"

"Still," Rosemary said, "I do hope Simon isn't overdoing things. He's got enough to put up with at home without having worries at work. I know Esther always exaggerates, but even so, I don't like to think of him looking ill."

I was able to judge for myself at the weekend when I went with Thea to collect Alice from the stables. As we drove up, a car parked beside us and Simon got out. He greeted us cheerfully and said, "It's such a beautiful day, I thought I'd have a ride and blow the cobwebs away. It's ages since I've been out."

"I didn't know you rode," I said.

"It would be difficult not to with Jo and Charlie around. They insisted on giving me lessons when I was practically a toddler! I'm not very good—nothing fancy, just a bit of mild hacking."

"Well," I said, looking appreciatively at his tweed jacket, boots and riding hat, "you're certainly properly turned out."

He laughed. "Jo wouldn't allow anything less."

We all went into the yard and looked down into the ring where Alice, now off a leading rein, was performing quite creditably with Liz.

"Is that your little girl?" Simon asked Thea.

She nodded. "Jo's idea, of course; she's a great enthusiast! But Alice loves it."

"Good for Alice," Simon said. He waved his hand and went off into the stables.

"Well," I said, "he looks all right to me."

"Who does?"

"Simon—Esther said she was worried about him and that he wasn't looking well."

"Oh, Esther! She's never happy unless she's got something to worry about. Simon's perfectly fine. Oh, Alice is coming in now; shall we go and meet her?"

That evening, when I was cooking Foss's fish in the microwave, I suddenly thought of what Esther had said about Simon looking worse after his holiday, and I wondered if he'd gone to London to try to get back with his girlfriend (What was her name? Annie? Rosie? something like that) and she'd turned him down. Perhaps he'd had enough of being the good son at home and wanted, at the age of—what was it?—thirtysomething, to get a life of his own at last. Certainly he's devoted himself to Esther and Gordon for a very long time. Not many young men of his age would have done as much.

The ping of the microwave put an end to these unprofitable thoughts. Foss, attracted by the smell of fish, suddenly materialized at my elbow on the worktop and Tris, who doesn't like fish, turned up nevertheless, knowing that I wouldn't dare feed one without the other. I put some fish into Foss's saucer and took it over to the tap to run a little cold water on it to cool it down. I removed Foss from the sink, where he had been keeping an eye on things, and put him and the saucer down on the floor. In response to Tris's impatient whine, I shook some dry food into his dish, gave a perfunctory squirt of air freshener to dispel the fish smell and took myself off to the sitting room for a quiet glass of sherry before I started making my own supper.

Rosemary and I set off in high spirits for our lunch together. It was a beautiful day and the drive across the moor to Lynton was especially fine with the moorland clothed in purple and gold.

"A real Mrs. Alexander day," I said to Rosemary.

"A what?"

"You know, the hymn 'All things bright and beautiful' . . . 'the purple-headed mountain' bit and all that. She wrote it when she was staying down here."

"Oh yes, at Dunster, wasn't it?"

"Yes—'The rich man in his castle, the poor man at the gate'—the verse we're not allowed to sing nowadays. Silly nonsense—I ask you, who's going to be offended by it? It's of its period. I mean, half of literature's politically incorrect if you look at it the wrong way!"

"I suppose so."

"Anyway, I always sing that verse silently under my breath when we have the hymn."

"It's very popular at funerals nowadays, have you noticed?"

"Yes, you're right—I suppose people think that, without *that* verse, it's sort of ecologically friendly!"

In spite of the good write-ups it had had, the restaurant wasn't very full, but we were early.

"They make a great thing about all the produce they use being locally sourced," Rosemary said, looking at the menu. "I suppose that's a good thing, unless you want an avocado. What are you going to have?"

"I don't know. I can never make up my mind until I know what other people are having. What are you?" I asked.

"I'll have the steak and ale pie," Rosemary said. "I'm getting very lazy about making pastry nowadays, so that will be a treat."

"I think I'll have the meatballs. I haven't had one for ages and homemade ones are very delicious. Mother used to do them for Father—he adored them—but I've never attempted them; they're really complicated to make. And a glass of wine, do you think?"

We gave our orders to the waitress and sat peacefully drinking our wine.

"Can you remember the name of Simon's girlfriend?" I asked Rosemary. "You know, the one who went to London. I was trying to think of it the other day."

"Oh, you mean Julie Phillips, Harold Phillips's daughter. Why?"

"I was just wondering why they broke up. They seemed very devoted and I thought they were on the verge of getting engaged, when she suddenly went away."

"I never really knew. I must say they did seem perfectly suited, so I was surprised. I believe they had a row about something and she went and got herself a job in London."

"It seems a bit drastic. What could the row have been about?"

"I don't know. I did ask Jack if he'd heard anything, but you know what men are like; they haven't any idea of what's happening right under their noses!" Rosemary said.

"It does seem a shame." I looked at my watch. "They're taking a long time with our food."

Eventually the waitress appeared with two of those large soup plates that are the trendy thing to serve food in nowadays and we looked at their contents in disbelief. The food was absolutely disgusting.

"Steak and ale pie be blowed," Rosemary said. "It's a ladle full of stew with a piece of puff pastry—

bought puff pastry," she said, trying a piece of it, "plonked down on top."

I poked at the small cannonball of brown, compacted matter sitting on a bed of lumpy mash, surrounded by grayish gravy. "Mine is even more horrible," I said. "I'm not even going to attempt it."

I waved the waitress over and asked for the bill. She looked at our untouched plates.

"Not worth waiting half an hour for," Rosemary said.

"I'm sorry," the waitress said. "Nobody's ever complained before. Would you like to speak to the chef?"

"I think that would be a waste of time," Rosemary said grimly.

Outside, we looked at each other and started to laugh. "So much for our treat!" I said. "Come on, let's go and get some fish-and-chips!"

Chapter Five

"I'm afraid it's going to be a good plum year," I said to Michael when he called to leave me some eggs. "The Early Rivers are quite ripe now—some of them are dropping—and the Victorias won't be far behind."

"We could come over at the weekend and help pick them, if that's all right," he said.

"That would be marvelous. I do hope Thea will be able to use a good lot of them. I suppose I'll have to make some jam. I'll try to make a bit of room in the freezer for the Victorias, but there are so many, and this year everyone will have plums and it'll be difficult to get rid of them!"

"Oh, I'm sure I can find some takers. Anyway, I'd better get off—I'm due back in the office."

"Thank Thea for the eggs—I'm so glad they've started to lay!" I said.

"Yes, she's really thrilled. Mind you, with the price of feed and corn, I suspect each egg will be worth its weight in gold."

"Still, better than a pan of fowl food on the stove. I can still remember the ghastly smell when I was a child and my aunt Edith kept chickens!"

"I can just remember her. She used to keep her hat on when she came to lunch with Grandma."

"Ladies did then. Extraordinary to think of it now."

The fruits of the earth are wonderful, of course, but when I contemplate the bowed-down plum trees and their harvest, soon to be followed by the apples and pears, not to mention the abundance of runner beans and courgettes, all clamoring to be picked *now*, then I do wish nature would arrange a decent interval between these things.

I was in the pet shop—well, it's more than that really, selling horsey things and feed for a variety of animals—looking at the notice board. It's always full of interesting things. Advertisements for horse boxes and hay and Muscovy ducks and chicken houses, alongside requests for ("good") homes for kittens ("two marmalade boys and a sweet tabby girl") and rescue dogs ("Patch—likes riding in cars") and notices of charity rides and dog shows. I was just considering a small poster that read ADVANCE NOTICE: MOUNTED GAMES WORLD PAIRS CHAMPIONSHIP when Jo came in and stood beside me.

"What is it?" she asked. "The double horse trailer or the retired greyhound?"

"Neither," I said, laughing. "I do rather long for a retired greyhound, but my two would never allow it! I love looking at these advertisements—such richness!"

"There's certainly a lot going on," Jo said. "That

reminds me, we're having an open day at the stables next Saturday afternoon. Is there any chance of Alice coming for a lesson then? I think it might encourage people to bring their young ones if they see her. I know it sounds a bit commercial, asking you like this, but I do really want to get as many people as possible interested. I just came in to put up a notice." She indicated a flyer in her hand.

"I think it's a splendid idea and I'm sure Alice will be delighted. She'd like to live at the stables if we'd let her!"

"That's marvelous. If you'd have a word with Thea, I'll ring her about times when I've got everything sorted out," Jo said.

"Fine. Oh, by the way, I don't suppose you'd like some plums. I've got a lot of really nice eating Victorias—it does seem such a shame to freeze them."

"Lovely. They're Charlie's favorite. He'll be delighted. We've got only apple trees and a few unproductive pears."

"Right, I'll bring them on Saturday, then."

As I knew she would be, Alice was thrilled at being part of the open day.

Thea was equally pleased though rather less vocal. "Michael keeps muttering about making Alice into a terrible little show-off," Thea said, "but I know he's delighted that Jo wants her there!"

I picked out the nicest plums for Charlie and took them along with me on the Saturday. There were quite a few people there, watching Delia and several other girls putting the horses over the jumps in one of the fields.

"They look pretty good, don't they?" Rosemary said. "Not exactly Horse of the Year Show, but quite professional."

"Absolutely splendid," I said. "I do hope it brings Jo in some more customers. Is Jilly here?"

"No, Alex has some sort of virus, so she's had to stay with him. They were afraid Delia might have caught it and wouldn't be able to come today. She's been driving them all mad about it, as you can imagine. Roger's here, though. He's actually got a weekend off." Rosemary's son-in-law, Roger, is now a police superintendent, so his work patterns are rather complicated. "He's over there talking to Charlie."

"Oh right—I'll just go and give him these plums. I'll see you in a minute."

Charlie was delighted with the plums and ate one right away. "My favorites," he said. "The nicest fruit there is and such a short season. Thank you, Sheila. They're wonderful."

"It looks as if the open day's a success," I said.

"Yes, we've had a few inquiries about livery and several bookings for lessons. I think it'll make a difference."

"Delia looks splendid," I said to Roger.

"I was just telling Charlie how grateful we are that she's taken to riding so enthusiastically," he said. "It makes her much more bearable to live with. I can't imagine how parents of other teenage girls survive!"

Just then Gordon Nicholson came up. He acknowledged Roger and me with a brief nod, but addressed himself to Charlie. "I want," he said, "to talk to you about Tarquin. What is your opinion of him? What is the situation—do we need to call the vet in?"

"It's only a slight case of laminitis," Charlie was saying as they went towards the stables. "We can cure it perfectly well by diet."

Roger and I moved away. "Tiresome man," Roger said. "I bet Charlie regrets taking that horse on for Dan Webster."

"I expect he felt he had to, since he's Gordon's friend and Gordon's Charlie's brother-in-law."

"I suppose so, but I bet they both want special rates. Gordon's always been very tight with money and I've no doubt he's told Dan that he can fix it!"

"Poor Charlie," I said. "He's too nice for his own good."

We'd joined Rosemary by this point and she added, "Goodness, yes. Gordon Nicholson is a ghastly man. Mother has all sorts of stories about his business dealings. I know Esther is a bore and a pest, but I can't help feeling sorry for her, married to a man like that!"

After a while Thea joined us and there were murmurs of appreciation from the visitors as Alice went round the ring on Cracker. "Oh look, isn't that *sweet*!" "What a dear little pony," "That little girl is riding it so well; isn't she clever!"

Thea looked at me and pulled a face. "Thank goodness she's too far away to hear any of that," she muttered, "or she'd be even more pleased with herself."

There was quite a storm in the night and it was still raining heavily in the morning. I was annoyed, though not surprised, to find a pool of water on the floor of the larder. That part of the house is a sort of extension, built in Victorian times. It has a slate roof, unlike the original structure, which is thatched. Some of the slates are loose and, when the rain falls from a certain direction, it comes through into the larder. I mopped the floor dry and put down an old saucepan to catch the drips. Whenever this happens I always remember Jane Austen, in one of her letters, bemoaning the fact that the rain had come into the storeroom and soaked everything—in her case it was a blocked gutter. *Plus ça change* . . .

Foss, who believes that no activity can be accomplished without his presence, came in and sat beside the saucepan, watching and waiting for each raindrop as it descended. I left him to it and went to ring Michael, who had promised a while ago to get a ladder and fix the slates.

"Only if you can spare the time," I said. "I know how busy you are at weekends. It'll be all right when the rain stops. It's just that I'm a bit worried about what will happen to the ceiling if it gets really saturated."

Michael, bless him, came after lunch. Fortunately

the rain had stopped, so I wasn't so worried about him climbing up a ladder and the slates being slippery.

"There now," he said, coming in again, "I think that's all right. A couple of slates had slipped, but I've got them fixed back securely. Any chance of a cup of tea?"

While we were having it, I said, "I'm so sorry you missed seeing Alice yesterday. Everyone said how good she looked on that pony!"

"I know, but it was the last match of the season, so I had to go. Not that I did much good—out for sixteen, cleaned bowled! But I've certainly heard all about it from Alice—at great length!"

I laughed. "Everyone did make a big fuss of her. But I know Jo was pleased. Apparently several people asked about children's lessons after they saw Alice's."

"Thea says that they—Jo and Charlie—are worried about money."

"Well, horses are expensive, you know—the upkeep. And I imagine there's a limit to how much you can charge, even the weekenders."

"They own all those fields, right up to the new plantation, don't they?" he asked. "Surely they don't need them all for pasture?"

"Probably not, and I believe they do rent out a couple. But I know Jo would hate to *sell* any of them."

"Anyway," Michael said, reaching for the last piece of shortbread, "they'd only get the agricultural price. You'd never get planning permission for land round there."

"I should hope not indeed!" I said, "and certainly Jo would never, ever consider it, however desperate they were."

"Well," Michael said with the optimism we all feel about affairs that don't immediately concern us, "I daresay they'll pull through. It's a perfectly good business as far as I can see."

"Perhaps," I said hopefully, "the open day will bring them in a lot more people."

One of the more irritating things in life is the sudden realization that you've lost a filling; it seems almost impossible not to keep poking at the hole with your tongue. Fortunately my dentist, Jim Robinson, had a cancellation and was able to see me the very next day. Jim is an old friend and a great gossip, which is fine, except that it's difficult to comment on the latest bit of news when your mouth is full of cotton wool, or you're poised to wince at the whirring of the drill and the unpleasantness of the water spray.

"We've got a new dentist coming soon," Jim said, poking experimentally at the hole in my tooth, "a South African—nice chap. It'll take some of the strain off Gordon Nicholson and me. Since old Waddell died, there's just been the two of us—not enough for a place the size of Taviscombe."

I mumbled something that I hoped would indicate appreciation of his position.

"And Gordon's not been putting in the hours,

from what I heard. Only there part of the week."
He applied the drill and April, his assistant,
sprayed water vigorously onto the tooth. "Do you
know a chap called Dan Webster? Have a rinse
away."

Given this respite, I said, "I think I've met him
once or twice, but I can't say I know him. Why?"

"They say he and Gordon are involved in some
sort of business deal; I don't know what."

"Really? I haven't heard anything about that."

"I've heard Webster has just bought a big place
and some land up beyond Upper Barton—must
have cost a packet."

April handed him the stuff she'd been mixing,
and he poked the cotton wool rolls into my mouth
and began to fill the tooth.

"It's all a bit of a mystery," Jim said. "I mean, *is*
Gordon carrying on with the practice or is he going
in full-time with whatever this new thing is?" I
tried to express interest in this speculation by raising my eyebrows, though I don't think he noticed.
"This Webster fellow, I think he's into property in
some way and Gordon's on the council; that may
be something to do with it!"

He took out the cotton wool, and I rinsed away
the bits of filling before saying, "Oh, I don't think
Gordon would do anything underhanded; he's always been a terrific one for abiding by the rules. A
real sea green incorruptible!"

Jim looked startled and I said, "You know, the
French Revolution—Robespierre, or at least I think
it's Robespierre. . . . No, I can't believe Gordon

would do anything wrong that's connected with his council work; he cares too much about his position as a councillor."

"True," Jim said thoughtfully, "*and* he's president of Rotary this year. He certainly wouldn't get involved with anything that might jeopardize that. Still, I would like to know what he's up to, especially with this new man coming; I need to know where we all are. Right, then, that's you sorted out. Don't bite on it for a couple of hours."

After I left the surgery I felt the need for a little quiet relaxation, so I drove down, past the harbor, to the end of the seafront. To my annoyance, the council has decided in its wisdom that the seagulls might annoy the visitors, so it has caused the railings where the seagulls have always perched to be treated with some noxious substance to keep them away. Of course it doesn't. They (the seagulls) perch on the shingle, rising in a noisy crowd whenever they spot someone who (in defiance of the notice posted by the aforementioned council) might have come to feed them. But I miss the line of gulls—neat little terns and large bully-boy herring gulls—alert and interested, occasionally making little forays, but returning to keep an eye on the passersby, waiting to see what they might offer.

I stood by the rails, looking out to the sea, and considering what Jim had said about Gordon and Dan Webster. I didn't believe that Gordon, however greedy he might be for money, would risk the position and reputation he's built up over the years. He likes being a big fish in a small pond, and his position on the council, and on the committees of other organizations, means a lot to him. He loves the idea of making rules for other people (it wouldn't surprise me if the seagull embargo was his idea), extending the sort of control he believes he exercises over his own family to the public at large.

Of course, it's possible that whatever Dan Webster wanted from Gordon was perfectly above-board and honest. But I couldn't really think of anything Gordon might have or do that could be valuable to an entrepreneur (for want of a better word) like Dan Webster. Gordon was comfortably off, but he didn't have the sort of money that would make him a possible investor in a really big project.

Looking out over the sea I saw threatening black clouds darkening the horizon. The gulls on the beach, apparently sensing the approaching storm, rose all together and flew off round the corner of the bay, and the first large drops of rain drove me back into the car. By the time I got home it was raining heavily and the sky was really dark. When I'd fed the animals, I made myself a light supper of steamed fish and mashed potatoes, because of my new filling, and sat down with it in front of the television. But the lights flickered from time to time and the rumble of thunder seemed to be getting nearer. Tris, who hates thunderstorms, sat pressed close by my feet and quivered at each lightning flash.

I went to bed early, taking the animals with me.

Tris lay on the bottom of the bed, making little whimpering sounds when the noise of the thunder was too much for him. Foss, who loves excitement of any kind, inserted himself behind the drawn curtains on the windowsill, where he watched the storm with the interest of a small child at a firework display. I couldn't get to sleep and lay there in the dark, not even able to see the time because the brief power cuts caused by the storm meant that my electric clock was affected and was now flashing madly on and off. After a while I put on the light, switched off the clock and looked at my watch. It was only just after midnight. With a sigh I picked up my copy of *Pillars of the House* and immersed myself in the lives of the Underwood family until the storm had passed over and I was able to sleep.

The next morning I had hoped to have a little lie-in, but now that the storm was over the animals were anxious to get on with their lives and saw no reason to be diverted from their usual regime, so we were all downstairs by eight o'clock, they with their bowls of food and I with a very necessary cup of coffee. When I went to let them out, I saw it was a beautiful morning and last night's raindrops were sparkling in the sun.

Inspired by the brightness and freshness of the morning, I had a great clear-out in the kitchen, sweeping away the detritus of daily living from the work-top—all the packets of dry animal food, a dish of withered apples and overripe bananas, a bowl half full of drippings I'd meant to put out for the birds, a packet of biscuits and a couple of storage tins that should have been put away in the larder, and the animals' antiflea spray—and wiped down every surface I could reach. After all that, averting my eyes from the cooker, I made myself another cup of coffee and had a nice sit-down with the daily paper.

It was late afternoon when Rosemary rang. Her voice was a little unsteady.

"Sheila, the most awful thing has happened. Charlie's dead."

Chapter Six

For a moment I didn't take in what Rosemary was saying.

"Dead?"

"Yes, but it's worse than that, Sheila. He's been killed."

"Killed," I echoed stupidly.

"In the stables. He was hit over the head—it looks like a burglary that went wrong."

"That's—that's horrible! When was this?"

"This morning—very early on. Simon rang a little while ago to tell me."

"What happened?"

"Apparently he got up when it was just light to see to the horses—they'd been restless in the night . . . that awful storm. Liz had the same idea and she arrived early. She went into the office to put her things down before going to see to the horses and she found him there. He was slumped on the desk and there was this awful wound on the side of his head."

"Oh no!"

"She said there was a very faint pulse—you know Jo made both girls do that first aid course—

so she rang for an ambulance straightaway and then she rang up to the house to let Jo know what had happened."

"Poor Jo. How could she bear it?" I asked.

"Liz said she was very calm and when the ambulance arrived, she went with him, of course. But he died on the way to the hospital without regaining consciousness."

"Where's Jo now?"

"At home. She rang Simon and he fetched her from the hospital. He'll stay with her tonight."

"Thank goodness for that."

"The police were all over the place. Apparently the safe—you know that small safe in the office—was open but the money, yesterday's takings, was still there, so I suppose whoever it was panicked when he saw what he'd done and ran away."

"Oh dear," I said wearily, "what a terrible waste of a wonderful life."

"I know. Charlie of all people, so kind and bright and intelligent and—oh, everything! It doesn't bear thinking about."

But, of course, it was all I could think about that evening. I knew the sort of numbness that Jo must be feeling, the denial and the feeling that somehow it should be possible to turn back the clock and make everything all right. And I knew, too, the pain of waking up each morning and realizing all over again the awful fact of death, and the terrible emptiness. But when Peter died, I had Michael, still quite young, someone I had to make an effort for, someone to give some sort of meaning to my life. Jo had no children. True, Simon was devoted to her and she to him, but it wasn't, couldn't ever be, the same.

Rosemary rang again next morning. "I wish I knew what to do about Jo. I'd like to go and see her, but I suppose it's too soon?"

"I think she'd like some time on her own," I said. "In a little while I'm sure she'll be glad to see people, but not just yet."

"I'm sure you're right; it's just that one wants to *do* something. Anyway, she's got Simon. Oh, I do hope Esther doesn't go rushing round! Though I'm sure Simon can keep her away. Poor Esther, I know she'd mean well, like we all do, but I know the last thing I'd want in these circumstances would be Esther wittering on."

"The last thing!"

"Do Michael and Thea know?" Rosemary asked.

"I rang them. They were dreadfully shocked and upset. Charlie meant so much to everyone, even people who didn't know him that well. Michael's their solicitor, so he'll be involved, though I suppose if there's a police inquiry, it won't be for a while."

"When I rang Jilly last night I had a word with Roger. Of course, he'd heard officially. He says Bob Morris will be looking into it, being the man on the spot. Bob's got his promotion, Roger said—he's an inspector now."

"Oh, that's good. Bob's a nice person, very sympathetic and kind. If anyone's got to talk to Jo about all this, I'm glad it's him."

The following morning I ran into Liz as I was coming out of the chemist and was able to ask her how Jo was.

"She's being marvelous," Liz said. "Well, you know Jo. She's dreadfully upset—you can see that—but she's trying to carry on as usual."

"I suppose you've got to when there are animals around," I said.

"Peggy and I can cope, but she says she needs to keep busy."

"I don't suppose it helps to have the police around asking questions."

"They've been pretty good. Bob Morris is nice. His daughter rides with us, so he knows his way around the stables—that helps. And knowing Charlie and Jo too."

"Of course." I hesitated. "What exactly happened?"

"I turned up at the stables early because I thought the horses would be spooked by the storm. I went straight to the office and that's where I found poor Charlie. It was so awful. It was . . ." Liz stopped and shook her head as if she couldn't say any more.

"I'm sorry," I said. "I shouldn't have asked you."

"No, it's all right." She paused for a moment and then went on. "He was lying across the desk and there was this terrible wound on the side of his head. They think he was hit with an iron bar or something. Can you believe anyone would do a thing like that? He was alive, but only just. I rang for the ambulance and they were very quick, but—but he didn't make it to the hospital, poor Charlie."

There were tears in her eyes and I put my hand on her arm. "I'm so sorry," I said. "We all loved him."

She nodded. "Everybody did. I can't imagine what it will be like there without him. And all for nothing—not even for the money. He'd opened the safe, the door was open, but the money was still inside. We usually take it out in the evening, when we close down, but that time we were busy and Charlie said leave it and I'll see to it in the morning. If only . . ."

"I know."

"The horses knew something had happened," Liz said. "It wasn't just the storm; they were so restless, I'm sure they knew."

"Certainly, if someone had been prowling around they'd have been upset."

"Yes, that's right. Anyway, I must get on. I came out only to get some paracetamol for Jo. She's got a rotten headache and we've run out."

"Give her my love. I'll be round to see her soon, but I didn't want to intrude."

"I think she'd like to see you—anyone who knew Charlie—you know."

It's peculiar, really; some days you can go round the shops and never see anyone you know, but other days you bump into several people all in one morning. In quick succession I saw Thea (on her way to pick up Alice from her friend Emma's), Anthea (who wanted me to fill in for Maureen at the next coffee morning) and, finally, Rosemary, who said, "Come and have some lunch at the Buttery. I'm absolutely shattered. I've just been taking Mother to buy a new pair of shoes and you can imagine what *that* was like!"

"Did you find any that she liked?"

Rosemary gave a hollow laugh. "What do you think!"

"Difficult?"

"Difficult. The floor of the shop was *strewn* with shoes and the poor girl—it was Shelley, you know, Mrs. Carter's daughter—was at her wits' end but trying desperately to be polite." She sighed. "I doubt if I'll ever be able to enter that shop again!"

It was quite early when we got to the Buttery and not too crowded.

"I'm going to have soup and an *enormous* piece of chocolate gâteau," Rosemary said. "And I'll be obliged if you'll have the same so that I can be indulgent without feeling guilty."

"Actually, I could do with a little indulgence myself," I said. "I saw Liz earlier on and asked her about poor Charlie. It was awful; she was very upset—so I feel the need of a little something myself."

We carried our trays down to the far end of the room where it was quiet.

"Did Liz say how Jo is?" Rosemary asked.

"Coping, of course. Carrying on as usual, as you'd expect. Liz thinks it would be all right to go to see her. Actually, Alice has a lesson on Saturday—I don't imagine they'll have canceled it—so I'll just go along then. Why don't you come too?"

"Yes, that would be best."

"I wonder when the funeral will be," Rosemary said.

"I suppose there'll have to be a postmortem, after the way he died, so I don't expect it'll be for a while."

"I imagine Simon will help her make all the arrangements. He's been so good, like a son to her—better than some sons, actually—and I'm so glad she's got someone like him to support her." She broke off and muttered, "Oh no!"

Esther's voice behind me said, "I thought I saw you two lurking down here. Do you mind if I join you?" Without waiting for an answer (and what answer could there be?), she put her tray on the table, moved my shopping bag from the spare chair and sat down.

"I don't often come here; I mean, it's just snacks really, not proper food, isn't it? But I had to do some shopping and get Gordon's suit from the cleaners, and I've got an appointment with Mr. Davis about my new glasses at two thirty, so it didn't seem worthwhile going home. Oh dear, the pastry on this quiche is very hard. I don't think I can eat that! Perhaps I should have had the soup like you—what is it?"

"Onion and potato," I said. "It's homemade and very good."

"Oh, I can't eat anything with onion. It gives me dreadful indigestion; the same with garlic. In a restaurant, whatever they may say, I can tell in a moment if there's even a *whiff* of garlic in anything!"

Esther settled herself more comfortably and began picking at the quiche. "So, wasn't it dreadful about poor Charlie! Of course, the moment I heard—Simon rang me—I went round straightaway." Rosemary and I exchanged glances. "I mean, I had to see if there was anything I could do for Jo. The police had gone when I got there, but there was still all that tape stuff they put round things. I was going up to the house—well, I thought Jo would be resting, I mean, after a shock like that, but, do you know, she was there in the stables seeing to the horses!"

"Well," I said, "when there are animals . . ."

"But she's got those two girls for all that sort of thing."

"She probably wanted to keep busy," Rosemary said, "to keep her mind off things."

"I don't see how mucking out stables would take your mind off a dreadful thing like that! No, I said to her, 'You should be lying down. You go up to the house and I'll make you a nice cup of tea.' But she said Peggy had just made some and would I like a cup. Just as though nothing had happened." She pushed her plate to one side and drank a little of her coffee. "No, what it is, she's in denial—that's what they call it now, isn't it? She can't bring herself to face up to it. Well, it's not surprising—Charlie was her life, really; she gave up her career for him, after all. If she'd gone on in the theater she'd have been a dame by now." She paused for a moment to allow us to take in the magnificent implications of this fact. "Still, I suppose they were happy, or as happy as anyone is nowadays."

"Oh yes," I said, "they were very happy."

Esther spooned some sugar into her cup and stirred it vigorously. "This coffee's very strong. No, what I mean to say is that she only took up all this horse business because of Charlie and now she can give it up. After all, she's seventy-four—quite a bit older than me, and, goodness knows, I get tired sometimes. All this hard work, looking after all those horses, is heavy work and too much for someone that age."

"She couldn't bear to give up," Rosemary said. "The stables are her life, just like Charlie was; they'll mean everything to her now that he's gone."

"That's all very well, but she'll have to give up sometime. From what I hear, those stables are practically running at a loss."

"That's as may be," Rosemary persisted, "but she'll carry on to the bitter end if need be."

"Anyway," I said, "there's every chance she can turn things round. She's got a lot of new people coming for lessons and livery."

"Yes, but now Charlie's gone," Esther said,

"she'll have to get someone to replace him, and that will cost money."

"You couldn't replace Charlie," I said sadly. "But I'm sure she'll manage. Liz and Peggy are splendid girls and she has a lot of voluntary help from all those horse-mad youngsters, and, of course, Simon is a great help."

"Oh, Simon—he's always up there. It's that or work," Esther said. "I often say to him he ought to be getting out more, but, of course he never listens to me. Boys are so difficult. Not that Vicky is much better. Thinks of nothing but work. She's in America now. Simon rang her to tell her about Charlie, but she can't get back for the funeral. You'd have thought a family crisis like that would come first, but she said she's on a deadline, whatever that may mean."

"If she's in America," Rosemary said, "she might not be able to get a flight anyway. Of course, we don't know when the funeral's going to be, and the postmortem will hold things up."

"It's perfectly awful," Esther said, "all this business with the police and everything. It's bad enough for poor Jo without all this."

"And she's perfectly right," Rosemary said when Esther had gone. "It must make things ten times worse—churning up her feelings with every question, not being able to lay him to rest properly."

"I know. And if they do manage to catch the person who did this horrible thing, there'll be the trial and the whole business brought up all over again."

* * *

I collected Alice on Saturday afternoon and drove her to the stables. As she was getting her things out of the back of the car she said, "Gran, Delia said that Charlie was dead. Is he?"

"I'm afraid so, darling."

"So we won't see him ever again?"

"I'm afraid not."

She considered this for a moment. "That's sad," she said.

I was pleased to see that the stables seemed to be as busy as usual, with quite a few people about and Liz and Peggy leading out the horses and adjusting the girths, just, as Esther said, as if nothing had happened. I looked around for Jo and saw that she was in the yard at the back of the stables, bent over the engine of their ancient Land Rover. In addition to her other skills, Jo is also a useful amateur mechanic.

Just then Rosemary arrived with Delia, who immediately took charge of Alice and led her off to the stables. We heard her say, "It's all right, Alice. I can tack up Cracker for you if Peggy's busy."

Rosemary smiled and I said, "Alice thinks she's wonderful; it's 'Delia says this' and 'Delia says that' all day long."

"We're just grateful—especially Alex—that Delia's got someone else to boss around!"

Just then they came out and we watched while Delia helped Alice to mount and then spent a long time meticulously checking the girth and adjusting the stirrups. Finally she took hold of the bridle and led the pony off into the ring, then handed her over to Peggy.

"Very professional," I said. "No, really, she's quite excellent."

"She says she doesn't want to do A levels and go to university—just wants to work with horses. We're hoping she'll grow out of it!"

"Well, there are horse management courses at some universities, I believe."

"Oh well, there's plenty of time yet." She looked around. "Have you seen Jo?"

"She's round the back fiddling with the Land Rover. What do you think—shall we go and have a word, or shall we leave it till later?"

"Oh, let's go now, I think, don't you?"

As we walked slowly towards her, Jo looked up and, wiping her hands on a piece of rag, slammed shut the bonnet of the Land Rover.

"Hello, you two," she greeted us, smiling.

"You look busy," I said.

"Oh well, got to keep the old girl on the road for a bit longer."

"Jo," Rosemary said, "we're so very sorry about Charlie. Such a terrible thing to have happened, especially a brutal attack like that . . ."

Jo shook her head. "No," she said, "it wasn't. We've had the postmortem report and it turns out that it was an accident after all."

Chapter Seven

At first neither of us spoke. Then Rosemary said, "What do you mean? How could it be an accident?"

Jo opened the back door of the Land Rover and threw the piece of dirty rag inside.

"It's complicated," she said, "but we've more or less managed to piece together what happened. The postmortem showed that the injury was caused by a horseshoe. It had to be Tarquin—we examined his feet and found traces of blood."

"But how . . . ?" I said.

"Charlie was worried about the horses after that storm, so he went down to the stables very early, while it was still dark. He went into the office to switch the lights on—that was probably when he opened the safe, since he'd been going to bring the takings back to the house—and then went in to see Tarquin, who he knew would have been the one most upset by the storm. Tarquin would have been restless—nervous from the storm and uncomfortable with the laminitis that affects his feet. Charlie would have bent down to examine them and, in doing so, knocked over a bucket—we found it rolled over to one corner of the stall. That, on top of everything else, must have startled Tarquin so that he reared up and caught Charlie a blow on the side of the head."

"But how did he get to the office?" I asked.

"Apparently it's perfectly possible to move after a blow to the head. It doesn't necessarily affect you straightaway. So he probably got up and went into the office to phone for help and then—then collapsed."

Her voice shook slightly and Rosemary said quickly, "Oh, Jo, I'm so sorry. This must be awful for you, to go over it like this."

Jo shook her head. "No," she said, "it's all right. Somehow when I talk about it, it doesn't seem as if I'm talking about Charlie, just some other person. And really, you know, it's such a blessing."

"A blessing?" I asked.

"Yes. When I thought he'd been killed by someone, deliberately and violently, that was almost the worst thing of all. Do you see what I mean? Charlie—who loved everyone and whom everyone loved—it seemed a sort of negation of all he'd been, his whole life, a *terrible* ending to it. But now I can accept it for what it was, an accident that could have happened to anyone."

"Will you get Dan Webster to take the horse away?" Rosemary asked.

"No, why should I? It wasn't Tarquin's fault; he didn't *mean* to do it. Actually, we've been making a lot of progress with him. He's a good horse at bottom; it's just that he hasn't been treated properly.

Liz has been working with him and he's taken to her very well. I really believe we can get him sorted out. Charlie would have wanted us to try, anyway."

"Well," Rosemary said, "I think you're being marvelous. I don't know how you can be so strong."

Jo smiled. "You carry on. The stables mean—meant—a lot to Charlie and me. It's never been just a business. It's the people and the horses and—oh, I don't know—the whole way of life, I suppose. He wouldn't want me to let everything go, now would he? Talking of which, I'd better get on; I've got a class waiting for me. See you later perhaps."

She moved away, down to the lower ring where Liz was putting up the jumps.

"She is amazing," Rosemary said. "Not getting rid of the horse and everything. How could she do it?"

"Well, I understand about the horse," I said, "and about being glad that it was an accident, but I do admire the calm way she goes about things."

"She's never been one to show her feelings, of course. I don't know how these things work, but I suppose all that sort of thing went into her acting."

"Oh yes," I said, "there was plenty of feeling there. Do you remember the way she spoke the willow cabin speech in *Twelfth Night* and the 'patience on a monument' bit? So moving!"

"And the young girl in *The Seagull*, goodness, that was fantastic. She was really brilliant. I can't imagine how she could bear to give it up!"

"Oh well. Charlie. It was a—what's the phrase?—a *coup de foudre*. She was simply bowled over by him, and stayed that way to the end. That's why it's so extraordinary that she's taking it so well."

We moved back towards the stables as Alice was coming back on Cracker.

"Gran, Gran, did you see me? Can you watch me dismount? You take *both* your feet out of the stirrups at once and then you get off like this!"

Peggy led the pony away as Delia appeared from the stables and said to Rosemary, "Can I stay for an extra hour? Liz said I could help her mix the feeds and fill the hay nets."

"I'm sorry, darling; I've got to be back before four," Rosemary said. She turned to me. "Mother's expecting me. She's got these two old chums coming to tea and I promised to take her some cream for the scones."

"Oh, Gran!" Delia said. "They're so busy here with it being a Saturday and they do need some help, especially now that Charlie . . ."

"It's all right," I said to Rosemary, "I can wait and take Delia back. I'll just give Jilly a ring and say we'll be a bit later. And you'd better go. Mustn't keep your mother waiting for the cream!"

Rosemary pulled a face and went.

On the way back in the car later on, I said to Delia, "What exactly *is* laminitis?"

She considered for a moment. "It's something that usually affects ponies, but some horses are subject to it. It's often caused by the horse eating too much new sweet grass in the spring, or the second growth at this time of the year. That's probably how Tarquin got it before he came to us. It causes a painful burning sensation in the hooves, which are very sensitive. You cure it mainly by diet and medication and also by poultices. I expect that's what poor Charlie was going to do when he was looking at Tarquin's hooves."

"Goodness," I said, "aren't you knowledgeable!"

"Oh, I've got a lot of books about horse management and horse diseases," Delia said. "It's very interesting. Actually, Tarquin's getting much better. Liz has put special boots on him—that helps, you know—so he should be quite all right soon. Liz says that Jo might buy him from Mr. Webster. I hope she does. I don't think Mr. Webster really likes horses and he hardly ever rides Tarquin—not that he could now with the laminitis, but before. I think he just wanted a good-looking horse to show off—that's what Liz says anyway."

I thought about what Esther's reaction would be to the news that Jo had bought the horse that had killed her husband, but then Esther would never allow Simon and Vicky to have a pet animal when they were children "because of the hairs all over the furniture."

"Liz is very good with Tarquin. She knows a lot about all sorts of horsey things." Delia turned round to address Alice. "She says she thinks you're getting along very well and perhaps you might be able to go out on one of the shorter rides soon. If you do, I'll come on that one with you—though, of course I usually go on the two-hour ones—and I can keep an eye on you. I expect you'd like that."

Overcome by this magnificent prospect, Alice, most unusually robbed of speech, nodded silently.

The church was full for Charlie's funeral. Not just local friends, but people from the horse world so eminent that even I recognized them. There was a general buzz of conversation, almost as if it were a social occasion. Charlie would have liked that. I went with Thea and Michael (lawyers always seem able to get time off for funerals) and when Rosemary came in she sat by us.

"Such a lot of people!" she whispered, "but I suppose he *was* such a well-known figure. So nice to think that people haven't forgotten him."

I was pleased to see, in the little procession that followed the coffin, that Simon, Liz and Peggy were gathered round Jo—her chosen family really—while Esther and Gordon walked separately behind. I was pleased too that Jo had chosen the proper *Book of Common Prayer* service. The beautiful language, soothing and familiar, felt so much more fitting to me than the determinedly cheery language of some contemporary services, though I suppose many people do find comfort in them. Horses for courses, as Charlie would say.

It was a surprise, though, to find that one of the hymns Jo had chosen was Newman's "Lead, Kindly Light." With so many people filling the church with their singing, the words came through with a freshness and immediacy.

I loved the garish day, and, spite of fears,
Pride ruled my will; remember not past years.
So long thy power hath blest me, sure it still
Will lead me on
O'er moor and fen, o'er crag and torrent, till
The night is gone.

Was that a summing up of Charlie's life? I hadn't thought of Jo as having a strong faith. I couldn't remember seeing her in church, though of course, Sunday is always a busy day at the stables. But maybe she has something of that splendid Victorian certainty, different from the vague hope that is the most many of us feel. Perhaps she really believes that one day she and Charlie will be reunited in some celestial city. I hope so.

Afterwards, when we were gathered with drinks and sandwiches in the local hotel, talking affectionately of Charlie, the atmosphere was definitely partylike. There was a buzz of chatter, with sudden little bursts of laughter as one person after another recalled some anecdote or incident. "I remember when . . . ," they began, and Charlie's life seemed to unroll from their memories of him.

Looking round, I saw Jo standing on her own at the table where the drinks and things were laid out, and I went over to speak to her. She was pouring herself a cup of coffee and looked up as I approached.

"I think it went well," she said.

"It went wonderfully, and now," I said, nodding

towards the room full of people, "it's turning into a splendid party."

Jo smiled. "He'd have been so pleased. He loved to see people enjoying themselves." She looked around. "I was very touched that so many people came, and a lot of them from the old days. Dear Charlie, it's wonderful that they still remember him. . . ." Her voice broke a little and the cup rattled in its saucer as her hand shook. She put it down quickly on the table and said, "I'm sorry, Sheila. It's been rather an emotional time." She laid her hand on my arm. "Thank you for coming," she said, and moved away.

As Michael, Thea and I were about to leave, Simon came over and spoke to us.

"It was a good turnout, wasn't it? I'm so glad for Jo's sake. She's been wonderful, of course, but it's all been so complicated, determining the cause of death and all that confusion. Thanks, Michael, for dealing with all the legal stuff—much appreciated. Now we must try to carry on."

"How are things at the stables?" I asked.

"Quite good really, in the actual day-to-day running of things. Liz and Peggy are brilliant and I try to put in a few hours when I can, just helping out—as well as doing the books and so forth. Jo, of course, is fantastic—never stops. I worry about her sometimes, but I do see that's what keeps her going. And we're all determined to keep up the standard; Charlie would have expected that." Simon smiled. "And we feel that somehow he's still in charge."

*   *   *

I'd arranged to have lunch with an old school friend, Rhonda Jackson. She lives quite a long way away in Devon, so we usually meet halfway at South Molton. We met at one of the restaurants that seem to have sprung up in the small market town now that a large number of fashionable Londoners have bought second homes down there. This one is in a mews behind the main street and has made a feature of its original stables origin. The menu is equally fashionable.

"What on earth are pumpkin gnocchi?" Rhonda demanded. She's always been very forthright and has what someone once described as the sort of voice that lost us the Empire, so that heads were turned in our direction. "And young leaves of *what*?" she went on.

"I quite fancy the crusted sea bass with celariac puree," I said.

"I shall have the fish cakes," Rhonda said, "though why they have to be Thai with chili dip beats me! Anyway, how're Rosemary and that terrible old mother of hers?"

I gave her the latest Taviscombe news and, of course, she wanted to know all about Jo and Charlie.

"Such an extraordinary thing to have happened," she said. "I never did trust horses. Enormous brutes—stand on your feet as soon as look at you! And I never understood about Jo. I mean, there she was, acting at the National and the RSC, on top of her profession, traveling all over the world—a wonderful life. You could have knocked me down with a feather when I heard she'd thrown it all up and gone back to Taviscombe of all places!"

"It was her home," I said mildly.

"But *Taviscombe*, such a dead and alive hole. I must say I couldn't wait to get out!" I refrained from commenting on the aliveness or otherwise of Newton Abbott, where Rhonda now lives.

"I must say it's always seemed a bit odd to me," she continued. "I wondered if there was something behind it all."

"What sort of thing?" I asked.

"Oh, I don't know—something to do with her career. You should know; you were always the one who was mad about the theater. Mind you, we never knew her really well in the old days, did we? She was a jump older than us. Now, *Esther* was still at school when we were. She was a prefect—do you remember?"

"Yes," I said with feeling, "I certainly do."

"Goodness, she was bossy—worse than the staff, really. I remember that time when Phyllis Shaw threw her school hat up onto the roof of the bus shelter while we were waiting for the school bus and Esther made her climb up to get it—said Phyllis had damaged the good name of the school!"

"I'd forgotten that," I said, "but I do remember how, when Rosemary and I sneaked off from that museum trip in Exeter to go shopping, she caught us coming back and meanly reported us to Miss Martin. Actually, Miss Martin was a good sport—

and I think would rather have liked to have gone shopping herself—and only gave us an order mark."

"Still," Rhonda said, prodding her fish cake experimentally, "I'm really sorry for poor Jo. Of course there are no children—that makes it much worse for her."

"Her nephew is very devoted to her," I said. "He lives in Taviscombe and has been marvelous over all this."

"I'm sure he has. But," she went on with the authority of the mother of four, "it's not the same as your own, is it? I don't know why they call this a *Thai* fish cake—it's only cod with bits in it."

"Jo's been wonderful," I said. "Carrying on as usual, though she must miss Charlie dreadfully; they were so close."

"I'd have thought she might sell up," Rhonda said, looking at the menu. "I think I'll go mad and have a pudding—that fish cake wasn't very filling. The pear and almond tart sounds all right. I can't be bothered to make pastry anymore. How about you?"

I shook my head. "Not for me. No, I'm sure Jo will never sell the stables; they're part of her life with Charlie. Anyway, I think it's the work that's helping her through."

"Oh well, it takes all sorts I suppose. But she's getting on a bit and it's hard work; she won't be able to carry on forever."

When I parted from Rhonda ("No really, you paid last time"; "Oh all right, but next time is on me"), I thought I'd drive back over Withypool Common. It was a beautiful afternoon, still bright, summer weather, though the heather was fading and tipped with brown, and the grass was no longer green and fresh, but dusty and close-cropped where the sheep had been feeding. Yet the sky was a light, clear blue and the sun felt warm through the windscreen of the car.

Considering it was still the school holidays, there wasn't much traffic, and very few people had stopped in the lay-bys on the hill. But, as I approached the turning that leads down to Landacre, I saw two cars parked on the verge: an old Land Rover and a smart new Mitsubishi four-by-four. Driving past, I realized that it was Jo's Land Rover, but there was no sign of her, nor of the other driver. Presumably she was seeing someone about a horse; it was a perfectly reasonable explanation. But the fact of seeing someone (or their car) in an unexpected place always evokes a faint prick of curiosity. I was puzzling about it until, out on the open moor, the sight of a large herd of ponies silhouetted dramatically against the sky drove all other thoughts from my mind.

Chapter Eight

A few days later I had to go up to Kirkby Lonsdale for several weeks. My cousin Marjorie had fallen and broken her arm rather badly, and her sister, Bridget, who lives with her and who would normally have been able to look after her, had gone to Australia to be with her daughter, who was expecting her first baby.

"It's frightfully good of you to offer, Sheila. I know she's got lots of friends and splendid neighbors," Bridget said, when she rang me from Melbourne, "but she really does need someone to monitor her insulin injections and, anyway, I'd feel *so* much better if there was someone actually sleeping in the house. I feel awful about being away just when she needs me, but Jenny's due any day now. . . ."

I took Tris with me, and Foss went to stay with Michael and Thea, to disrupt their household and tyrannize over their little cat, Smoke. In a way, I wasn't sorry to be going away. Somehow too much seemed to be going on in Taviscombe and I felt it would be nice to have a break and live in a completely different environment for a while. Marjorie and I always get on well and I was looking forward to being in the Lake District again.

At first Marjorie really did need a lot of attention and several visits back and forth to the hospital to adjust the horrible metalwork frame on her poor arm; it was a challenge to find garments she could wear and getting her up and dressed took at least half an hour. But after a while she was well enough to come out for little drives so that I could revisit my favorite places.

"It's wonderful to be out of the house again," she said as we sat looking out at the still waters of Coniston. "I was beginning to feel quite claustrophobic."

"You went to the hospital on Monday," I said.

"That's not *out*. I mean, just being a little bit back to normal."

"Do you feel like some tea?" I asked. "I seem to remember there's a nice place quite near here, if it's still open this late in the season."

"I meant to ask you the other day," Marjorie said as I buttered a scone and cut it up for her, "why your friend Jo gave up the stage like that."

"Well, she met Charlie. . . ."

"*Such* a pity! I remember seeing her at Stratford, years ago, when I used to take the English sixth to see their set plays when they were doing them there. What always struck me was how *different* she was."

"Different?"

"Well, you know how some actresses—and actors too—are always the same, always themselves, if you know what I mean. But she was always different in every part she took. When you saw her in *Twelfth Night* and then in *Hamlet*—well, they might not have been the same actress."

"Yes, I do know what you mean. I suppose it's just that she was a brilliant actress."

"I'll always remember her and James Carlyle in *Hamlet*. Now, he was a *marvelous* actor. But it was a most peculiar production; they made Hamlet absolutely selfish and self-obsessed, not sympathetic at all. She was wonderful as Ophelia. She did the mad scene so beautifully, but the bit I remember most was the nunnery scene with Hamlet. I've never seen anything so cruel and unpleasant as his rejection of her! I suppose it was all part of the production, and it was certainly very memorable—well, look how it's stayed in my mind all these years!"

"I never saw that production and I don't think I'd like an unsympathetic Hamlet."

"It certainly got my sixth form talking!"

"I did see James Carlyle's *Macbeth*," I said. "That was with his wife, Jane Neville. He was better than she was, very charismatic, but she wasn't really up to it. Splendid in light comedy, but she wasn't really a Shakespearean actress."

"Those husband and wife things don't always work when one is better than the other. Is there any more tea in the pot? I think I could manage another cup."

The weather was amazingly kind and we made other trips—to Thirlmere and Buttermere, Derwentwater and Ullswater—all full of happy memories for me. It was late in the season and there weren't too many people about (one always wishes that places like the Lake District could be conveniently emptied for the duration of one's visit), just the red and blue anoraks of the ramblers dotting the landscape in the distance or cramming onto the ferries at Windermere.

On my last day we went to Rydal Water and then on to Grasmere so that I could have another look at Dove Cottage.

"It's a good thing to have visitors," Marjorie said. "Somehow, left to yourself, you never go to places like this, on your own doorstep."

By a fortunate chance we had the cottage to ourselves, so I was able to wander round at will and picture not William but Dorothy Wordsworth walking many miles about the countryside in all winds and weathers with William, copying out William's poems by inadequate lamplight, keeping house for William in this uncomfortable, inconvenient cottage, with the added burden of frequent visits from Coleridge, not the easiest of guests. No wonder her diary often recorded, "Laid down with a headache."

"I suppose if you're very fond of someone," Marjorie said when I spoke of this, "you don't mind what you do or where you are as long as you're with them."

Bridget came home at last ("Yes, it was a boy, eight pounds and red hair! Jenny's fine. It was wonderful to see her and Greg and Andrew—

that's what they're calling him. You've been an absolute angel, Sheila, and I can't thank you enough."), and I was able to go home.

I must say I did feel better for the break.

"A change of scene," I said to Rosemary, "that's what they say, and I really feel as if I've had a holiday, though it was quite hard work with poor Marjorie. That awful metal contraption meant she couldn't do anything much. But she was very good about it all and it was nice to see her again, better on her own, really. I'm very fond of her and of Bridget, but somehow, not together. And, although Marjorie's house is very comfortable, there's nothing like your own bed, is there? So what's the news? Have I missed anything important?"

"Not really," Rosemary said, pouring us both another cup of coffee. "Mother's ignored my advice and is having her sitting room decorated after all. So she's living in the dining room and making life hell for poor Elsie and, of course, for poor little Mr. Burge who's *doing* the decorating—keeps changing her mind, all the usual things. She did hint that it would be more convenient if she came to stay with us while it was all happening, but I *totally* ignored that. Jack would have divorced me if I'd said yes! I think she knew that and didn't press it."

"Poor you! How about Jo? How is she managing?" I asked.

"Seems to be fine. Simon was up there quite a bit, but he's at home more just now because they're worried about Gordon."

"Worried?"

"Well, you know he's had a heart condition for years, and it seems to have got worse lately. But you know what men are like. Esther's been at him to go and see Dr. Macdonald and he kept putting it off. When he did finally go, Dr. Macdonald said he wanted him to see a specialist and have some more tests, but—it makes me so cross—Gordon says he's too busy at the moment and he'll think about it! So selfish when he *knows* how worried Esther is."

"We've always known he's selfish, but I'd have thought he'd want to have it seen to for his own sake."

"Oh, you know how they are—keep on saying that they're fine and get irritated when you try to persuade them to be sensible. Jack's just the same; he'll never do anything about his bad back. I've offered to make an appointment for him with that wonderful chiropractor Jilly found when my neck was so bad, but he tells me not to fuss, and then goes on moaning and groaning about it. I think he enjoys being a martyr."

"It can't be easy for Esther; I should think Gordon's difficult enough when he's well. I'm glad she has some support from Simon."

"I really think he's trying to do too much. He looked absolutely exhausted when I saw him last week. Poor boy, he does his best, but Gordon's disagreeable and Esther would drive anyone mad— and then there's his job. I think the time he spends up at the stables, however hard he may work there, is the only relaxation he gets!"

"Yes, it can't be easy. It all falls on him now that Vicky's in London."

"Oh, I nearly forgot," Rosemary said. "I thought I'd better warn you—Anthea's got this new idea for raising money for the kitchen at Brunswick Lodge."

"For heaven's sake," I exclaimed. "We had that new sink and they replaced the entire work-top only last year!"

"I know, but Anthea says we ought to have a dishwasher and a microwave."

"I agree about the microwave," I said, "and that would cost virtually nothing, but why do we need a dishwasher when we've got so many helpers? Anyway, it's mainly cups and saucers and glasses."

"Ah," said Rosemary, "*that's* Anthea's idea."

"What do you mean?" I asked warily.

"She wants us to do light lunches, so, of course, there'd be lots more washing up."

"At Brunswick Lodge?"

"Yes."

"She must be mad! Who on earth is going to cook them?"

"She says that people will cook things like shepherd's pie and lasagna—things that can be heated up in the microwave—at home, and then do salads and so forth at the lodge."

"Leaving aside the complete impossibility of organizing something like that, *who*," I demanded, "is going to be there every day to serve these lunches? For heaven's sake, it's difficult enough to find stewards and people to do the weekly coffee mornings!"

"I thought you wouldn't be keen," Rosemary said, laughing. "Anyway, don't be cross with me; I'm merely the unwilling messenger. As I said, I'm just warning you so that she doesn't take you by surprise!"

It's amazing, really, how much there is to do when you've been away. Little things like restarting the milk and the papers, and finding that you're out of basics like flour and marmalade, things you meant to get before you left and never did. And then there were the animals, of course. Although I knew from Thea that Foss had had a marvelous time with them, being thoroughly spoiled, sleeping on Alice's bed ("Poor, darling Foss, he's *lonely*"), bossing around Smoke and enjoying a feud with the large black cat next door, nevertheless, when I brought him home, he treated me as a monster who had cast him into exile. He remained aloof for several days, only approaching to pick disdainfully at the choicest foods I cooked for him by way of expiation. He wasn't much better with Tris, clouting him over the nose when his erstwhile playmate went to greet him and pointedly ignoring him for the rest of the day. Poor Tris, who, compared with a wily Siamese, is a simple soul, couldn't understand what he'd done wrong and cast anxious glances in my direction, asking for reassurance. But things got back to normal eventually.

I spent quite a lot of time vacuuming and polishing. It's amazing how dismal the house looks when you've been away—not dirty exactly, just a bit musty and generally neglected. I flung open all the windows (which Foss adored, coming and going as the fancy took him and startling me by suddenly appearing on unexpected windowsills) to let in the fresh air, which, now that summer was over, had a hint of autumn. For a few days I was too busy to do any real shopping but, when I was reduced to defrosting an undated package from the freezer that was labeled only CASSEROLE for my supper, I thought I really ought to go and stock up.

I was just on my way to see if I could find the tinned tomatoes when I saw Anthea at the other end of the aisle. I did a sharp U-turn to escape her and came face-to-face with Esther.

"Oh, you're back then," she greeted me. "Did you have a nice holiday?"

"Well, it wasn't a holiday exactly. . . ."

"The Lake District—it was the Lake District, Rosemary said, wasn't it?—is very nice, though I expect it was full of tourists. I believe it's what some call a honey trap. Gordon and I went a couple of years ago. Well, he had a patient who moved up there and who invited us both for a few days when we were on our way to Edinburgh when Gordon had to go to that conference."

"Really."

"They were very kind—Gordon's patients, that is—and took us around to see everything. Though to be honest, one lake is very like another, and when you've seen one you've seen the lot!"

"I was actually up there to look after my cousin who broke her arm rather badly. . . ."

"Oh, arms are so difficult, aren't they? It's easier with legs—I mean, with them you can't move about very well, but at least you can brush your teeth and comb your hair!"

"I know. . . ."

"I remember when Gordon broke his wrist— that was when he had that car accident years ago— he was absolutely helpless for ages. Such a performance *that* was!"

"How is Gordon? Rosemary said he hadn't been well."

"No, his heart's playing up again. He really ought to see a specialist—Dr. Macdonald was quite annoyed with him when he put it off—but he's been very seedy off and on for several weeks now. You know, one day he's fine, the next he's feeling really bad. He says it's all this medication he's on, those beta-blockers. He's always complaining about taking those—you get all these side effects. Anyway, I put my foot down and I made an appointment for him to see Dr. Macdonald next week to arrange things. It can't be before then because *he's* off on a conference; that's all doctors seem to do these days. Gordon was cross with me for going behind his back like that, but I think, although he wouldn't admit it, he was quite relieved."

"I'm so glad. I'm sure you did the right thing."

"Oh, you know what men are like—say they

don't want to make a fuss and then expect you to run around after them when it turns nasty. I know when Gordon had a bad cold last year he *would* go to a council meeting, even though it was a dreadful night, wind and rain and I don't know what. Of course he wouldn't listen to me, would he, and it turned into bronchitis and we had a terrible time of it."

"I know; they can be maddening. . . ."

"Simon's just as bad. He looks really off-color. I'm sure they're working him too hard at work, but he does try to do what he can for Gordon, doing the accounts and so forth and, now that Gordon's not too well, he's been doing some letters for him and writing up council notes, that sort of thing. I don't understand any of it, but I'm sure it must be a help."

"Rosemary said she thought Simon looked a bit tired."

"I keep telling him he's doing too much, but of course he doesn't take any notice of what I say."

"Boys don't really, do they?" I backed away and wheeled my trolley in the opposite direction. "I hope all goes well," I said as I made my escape.

What with dodging Anthea and trying not to reencounter Esther, it took me some time to do my shopping. When I got outside it was pouring with rain and thoroughly dismal, so I abandoned any idea of doing more shopping in the town and went straight home. After I'd unpacked my shopping (a job I hate) and had a bit of lunch, I felt restless. There were certainly things I *ought* to do—two books to be reviewed mutely reproached me from my desk—but somehow I couldn't settle to anything. I roamed about the house, annoying the animals (Tris had turned his back on the weather and was curled up in his basket; Foss was perched on the arm of the sofa, watching the snooker on television) and finally ended up in the kitchen.

On an impulse I decided to do some cooking—something detailed and fiddly that would occupy a lot of time. I put on the radio and got out the things to make a lemon meringue pie and began to measure out the flour to make the pastry. There is something satisfying about cooking something you don't *have* to. Grating the lemon rind and slowly and carefully stirring the egg and lemon mixture in the double saucepan were a positive pleasure, though they were tasks I normally found irritating. I whisked up the egg whites for the meringue, while lending half an ear to two men earnestly discussing a possible interest rate rise, but, important though I'm sure that was, somehow it seemed less important just then than achieving exactly the right consistency of soft peaks by my whisking.

After the pies were finished and baked, I regarded them with pleasure. I'd made enough for two and it gave me satisfaction to think that I would give one of them to the children who would really enjoy it (it was Thea's favorite). I felt a moment of pity for Jo who had no one now to make some special treat for, and for Esther, who would probably never even think of doing such a thing.

Chapter Nine

When I called to leave the lemon meringue pie for Thea, she greeted me eagerly. "Oh good, I was just going to ring you. Could you do me a favor? My washing machine's finally given up the ghost. Well, I say 'finally,' but we seem to have had it only a couple of years. I bought a new one, but they can only deliver it on Friday afternoon—and of course they can't give me an exact time—and Alice has a riding lesson then. So would you mind collecting her from school and taking her to the stables?"

"Yes, of course. And how maddening about your washing machine. Things simply don't last nowadays. What is it they call it—built-in obsolescence? I was just saying to Rosemary the other day, when my fridge packed up, that the one Peter and I had when we were first married lasted more than thirty years! No, it'll be lovely to see her. What time's the lesson?"

"Four thirty. Is that all right?"

"Splendid. I can take her back with me and give her a sandwich to keep her going, and if you give me her jodhpurs and things, she can change then. Are you all right for washing until Friday? Would you like me to take anything back and put it in my machine?"

"No, it's fine. Actually, it's quite a relief *not* to be able to do any washing for a bit. I'm always putting stuff into the machine, forgetting that it's simply piling up the ironing!"

Fortunately, Alice is still at the age when being fetched from school is perfectly acceptable (unlike Delia who, Rosemary tells me, regards being collected by any adult as a brutal attempt to embarrass her in front of her friends), and she greeted me with enthusiasm.

"Hello, Gran. Are you going to come and see me ride? Cracker really knows me now—he's so sweet—and Liz says I can go on a proper long ride soon. Have you got my things? *And* my crop—not that I need a crop with Cracker; he's so good."

When we arrived at the stables, although it was early, there was another car there. It was a Mitsubishi Shogun, like the one I'd seen out beyond Withypool parked beside Jo's Land Rover. Alice gathered her things together and, as we went into the stable yard, Dan Webster came out of the office. He turned in the doorway and I heard him say, "I'll stay in touch—you never know!" He greeted me with a wave of the hand, got into the Shogun and drove away.

Alice saw Peggy in one of the stables and ran off to join her. I sat on one of the mounting blocks, waiting for her to emerge. After a short while Jo came out of the office. She looked tired and not very well.

"Hallo," I said. "Are you all right?"

She smiled. "I'm fine. It's just been a tiring day, one thing after another; you know how it is."

"I saw Dan Webster leaving," I said. "Was he one of the tiring things?"

"In a way. I'm buying Tarquin off him, but there's some difficulty about the horse passport, silly bureaucratic nonsense, so it's all a bit complicated and, as I said, just one more thing!"

"I don't expect Dan Webster is the easiest person to do business with anyway," I said.

"Oh, he's quite keen to make the sale. I don't think he'd find many buyers; poor Tarquin has a reputation now, of course. Unfair, really, there's no vice in him; it's just that he was badly handled before he came here. Liz is doing a marvelous job on him. Anyway, I know that's what Charlie would have wanted."

"You're probably right," I said doubtfully.

"I'm sure I am." She smiled and, as several children in jodhpurs arrived, she looked at her watch. "I must be off. I've got a lesson. Nice to see you."

I dutifully watched Alice going round and round the ring under Peggy's careful eye, but my mind kept wandering to Dan Webster and what the meeting up on the moor had been about and what he had meant by "You never know."

We seemed to be having an Indian summer and, although I'd meant to put away all my summer clothes, it was still warm enough to keep on wearing them. This year at least, as Rosemary said, we're getting some *use* out of our summer things. In spite of being in the southwest, Taviscombe can be quite chilly. I can distinctly remember, when Michael was small, wearing a sheepskin coat one August day when I was watching him build sand castles on the beach. Still, I suppose if all they say about global warming is true, then we'll have no more use for our heavy sweaters and winter coats.

I'd just decided, as a compromise, to put away my summer dresses and keep out the skirts and tops, when the phone rang. It was Rosemary.

"Simon's just rung to say that Gordon died last night."

"Good heavens! I had heard that he wasn't well, but I'd no idea. . . . What was it, heart?"

"Yes. It was quite sudden. Of course, he should have been having those tests, or at least seeing Dr. Macdonald, but he kept putting things off."

"What happened?"

"He went off to a council meeting; apparently he seemed quite all right then. He was late back—they're used to that, but after a while Esther started to fret about keeping his supper hot, so Simon went out to see if he was coming and saw that his car was parked in the drive. He went out and found Gordon collapsed over the wheel. Simon phoned an ambulance, of course, but he was dead when they arrived."

"How awful—poor Esther!"

"I know. Simon says she's still in shock; doesn't seem to have taken it in."

"No, I'm sure one doesn't. Sudden death may be the most merciful way to go, but it's wretched for those left behind."

"Fortunately Simon's there to see to everything and Vicky's coming home from London."

"Has Simon told Jo?" I asked.

"Yes—he said it was difficult—you know, with Charlie just gone."

"Of course. They're both widows now, though I don't really think of Jo as a widow, do you? I feel as if Charlie's still there with her somehow."

"In a nice sort of way—yes, I know what you mean. A loving presence. Not like poor Gordon. Though," Rosemary added, "I don't know why I say poor Gordon. I disliked him when he was alive and the fact that he's dead hasn't changed my opinion of him."

"Poor Esther, though," I said. "She'll be lost without him. I don't think she ever made a real decision in her life—everything was referred to him."

"Poor Simon, if you really get down to it," Rosemary said. "He'll never be able to escape now—I mean, Vicky will be going back to London after the funeral, and then there'll be just him and Esther."

"I don't suppose you know when the funeral will be?"

"No, I don't think Simon's fixed it yet; it's still early days."

I rang Esther later that day, just to see if there

was anything I could do—though, goodness knows, there's little enough that anyone *can* do, or say, for that matter.

"That's very kind of you, Sheila," she said. She sounded somehow muted and uncertain. "I don't think there is. Simon's been very good and Vicky will be here tomorrow. I thought I ought to go to Taunton to get a hat. Well, I've got quite a nice one, but it's navy and that's not quite the same as black, is it? Though, of course I do have a navy coat. . . . but Gordon was very definite about things like that. He always wore black for funerals—not just a black tie, but a black overcoat, even in summer, over a dark suit. He said it was paying proper respect and he wouldn't like me not to. I've got a black coat. It's a lightweight summer coat, but it *is* black, and I've got a black-and-white silk dress— or do you think black and white wouldn't be suitable?"

"I think it would be fine," I said, "and I have a black hat if you'd like to borrow it. It would save you going all the way to Taunton. Actually, come to think of it, I've two black hats—one straw and one felt. I suppose the straw one would be better if you're wearing a summer coat. Anyway, I could bring them for you to try."

"Oh, would you, Sheila; that's very kind. But what about you?"

I didn't admit that I hadn't intended to wear a hat at all. "Oh, I've got a navy one—a very *dark* navy, so that would be all right for me."

I took the hats round the next afternoon and

found Esther less subdued, but still not really her old self. When we went up to her bedroom to try on the hats, I was touched to see that Gordon's pajamas were lying folded on one of the pillows and his hair brushes were still on the dressing table.

"What do you think, Sheila, will this coat do? It's quite full—what we used to call a duster coat, isn't it?" She went over to one of the wardrobes and took out the black-and-white dress for me to see. "Do you think this is all right? The coat will cover up the dress completely in the church, though I suppose I'll have to take it off afterwards at the—what do you call it? Not reception?"

"I don't know," I said. "The Irish say 'wake' of course, but it doesn't seem suitable in this case. People just say 'afterwards at' wherever it is."

"Simon thought the Westfield would be suitable. Gordon always says it's the best hotel in Taviscombe."

"Yes, that would be splendid. It's quite near the church, so everyone can walk there."

Esther sat down at the dressing table and tried on the hats.

"I think the straw one," she said, "or what do you think? The felt one is more off the face. I never did have the face for a hat. Jo did. She had a big Garbo hat in pink felt. It had a big brim that came down all one side of her face. I remember she said it made her look mysterious, whatever that might have meant. She had it all those years ago when she went off to London."

"I think the straw one will be better," I said.

"Yes, you're right; I'll wear that one."

I mentally noted that this was the first time in all our acquaintance that Esther had asked for my opinion and had actually taken it. "That's fine," I said, "but I'll leave both of them in case you change your mind."

She put the hats down and looked at them doubtfully; then she got up and said, "Shall we have a cup of tea?"

"That would be nice."

I followed her into the kitchen while she put the kettle on, and when the tea was made she said, "Shall we have it out here? Gordon doesn't like us to eat or drink in the kitchen. He says, 'What do we have a dining room for?'"

"I don't think a cup of tea counts," I said.

"Oh"—she moved over to one of the cupboards—"would you like some biscuits, or there's a cake I got from Stenners the other day, before . . . but it's been in a cake tin, so I'm sure it's quite fresh."

"No, really, just a cup of tea will be fine."

She sat down and poured the tea while I tried to think of something to say.

"Vicky's coming home tomorrow," she said.

"That's nice."

"She said she should be able to stay for a full week because she wants to see Jo about some program or other—but I'd have thought her father's funeral would be quite enough reason for staying."

"I expect she just wants to get her program

sorted out. I imagine she's under quite a bit of pressure in her job."

"I suppose so," Esther said absently. She was silent for a while and then she said quite suddenly, "I miss him so. I don't know what I'm going to do without him. How am I going to bear it, Sheila? How am I going to go on?" She was crying now, not sobbing, but quietly crying, tears pouring down her face.

I put my hand on hers. "You get used to it. No, that's not true; you never get used to it, but you learn to accept it. When Peter died, I was lucky to have Michael. You have Simon and Vicky; they'll get you through."

"If only he'd seen Dr. Macdonald, if *only* he'd listened to me—he might have been here now. He wasn't old; he had years ahead of him. It need never have happened; he could have had a bypass, a new heart, even. . . ." She fumbled for a handkerchief and wiped her eyes. "I'm sorry, Sheila, giving way like that."

"Don't be silly," I said. "It's good for you to give way. Here, drink your tea; it will make you feel better. Shall I stay with you until Simon comes home?"

"No, I'm all right. Anyway, I've got to get on with supper. I've got some nice lamb chops, Simon's favorite—and I thought I'd make an apple pie for tomorrow when Vicky comes. I don't suppose she does much cooking in that flat of hers."

Seeing Esther more or less restored to her proper self, I left and on the way home I thought about how the two sisters had each reacted to their sudden loss. I suppose it was inevitable that someone as erratic as Esther should have become vague and disorientated while Jo, the strong one, had collected herself quickly and, to all intents and purposes, got on with her life. I mentioned this to Rosemary when I met her in the library the next day.

"Well, considering how wonderful Charlie was, I think it's fantastic that Jo is coping so well," she said. "Of course, it helps to have to keep busy—the stables are a lot of hard work—and I expect she feels she's keeping things going for Charlie's sake. I suppose what I mean is that Jo and Charlie were partners in everything, whereas poor old Esther was completely under horrible Gordon's thumb. She had no sort of life of her own, did she? So she's got nothing to fill the gap."

"There's Simon and Vicky," I said. "Though, of course, they've always been sort of peripheral to her life and her devotion to Gordon. She'll be quite well off, I should think. Perhaps she could travel."

"Can you imagine it?"

"Well, no, not really, not unless she took Simon with her, and that would defeat the whole object of the exercise, which is somehow to arrange things so that Simon gets a life of his own."

"It's a pity Vicky lives in London."

"Oh, Vicky's the selfish one—and ambitious too. She wouldn't let any family feeling get in the way of her career. Esther was quite hurt that all she seems to be interested in, when she comes down for the funeral, is getting Jo to do some program or other."

"Poor Esther. Goodness, is that the time. Mother expects me at twelve and I haven't found a book for her yet. I'll have to take this life of the Queen Mother. I'm sure she's read it, but she's read so many of them she may not remember!"

Gordon's funeral was very different from Charlie's. The church was, indeed, quite full.

"Everyone on the council is here," Rosemary said, looking round, "and most of the Rotarians."

But the atmosphere was stiff and formal rather than warm and loving; people were here because they felt they *ought* to be, not because they wanted to be. I saw Dan Webster come in and make his way to a pew at the front, across the aisle from the one set aside for the family. He was the only person sitting there, most people having modestly crowded into the pews at the back.

"You're wearing a hat!" Rosemary said suddenly.

"I felt I had to," I said. "Esther was making such a thing about what sort of hat *she* would wear. It's really uncomfortable; it's pressing on my ear. Oh, here they come."

Esther came down the aisle with Simon, Vicky and Jo—I saw, without surprise, that she was wearing the felt hat, not the straw one—and the service began. There were several addresses by members of the council and other public bodies, all stressing the good works that Gordon had been associated with, so that I felt it was beginning to re-semble a company report rather than a funeral ser-vice. The hymn was "Abide with Me," which always makes me so choked up that I can't sing the words; Rosemary nudged me when we got to the line "Change and decay in all around I see," be-cause it's one of our favorite quotations.

Then it was all over and we trooped off down the road to the Westfield Hotel where a lavish buf-fet was set out, though I, for one, didn't feel like eating anything. Indeed, only the council members and other similar guests seemed inclined to do so. The men (and they were mostly men) piled their plates high and, with full glasses, retreated to the far corner of the room where they appeared to be embarked upon some sort of business meeting. Perhaps it was the most suitable thing to do, since I'm sure they were the ones who would miss Gordon most. Now it would be someone else who would make up a quorum, make a resolution or pass a motion.

"Here," Rosemary said, handing me a glass of wine. "We'll have a couple of these and then go and have a word with Esther."

I noticed that Vicky had cornered Jo and was talking to her earnestly. But Jo was standing there impassively, seeming to let the flood of talk wash over her. I smiled to myself, knowing that she would be more than a match for her niece and no amount of talk would persuade her to do anything she didn't want to do.

Esther was over by the door with Simon by her

side. We went across and said all those useless things one does on such occasions.

"I think it went off very well," Esther said.

"It was a splendid service," I said, "and the church was very full."

"Mr. Broadbank was there," Esther said. Mr. Broadbank is our MP. "He couldn't come on here because he had to get back to London—for the House, you know—but it was good of him to come. Gordon would have liked that; he did a lot for the party, of course. . . ." Her attention wandered as she saw someone else approaching, and she turned to greet them.

"Thank you for coming," Simon said. "Please call round and see her sometime. I know she'd appreciate that."

It was good to be outside in the fresh air.

"Come on," Rosemary said. "I snaffled a few of those not-very-nice sandwiches. Let's go down to the seafront and feed the seagulls."

Chapter Ten

It's always silly to shop on a Saturday if you don't have to. The supermarket checkouts are slower, the queue at the post office is longer and in the smaller shops the Saturday staff don't know where things are kept. I'd just decided to give up and go home when it suddenly started to rain quite heavily. Fortunately, I was quite near the Buttery, so I took shelter inside with a cup of coffee. A lot of people had had the same idea and it was very crowded. I was standing for a moment with my cup held insecurely in a hand already weighed down with shopping bags, when I heard someone call my name. It was Simon beckoning me to join him and his sister, Vicky.

"Oh, thank you so much," I said, putting my cup down and prizing off the handles of the bags that were now cutting into my fingers. "It's not usually quite as crowded as this, but the rain has driven everyone indoors."

We spoke for a while about the funeral and I asked Vicky how long she was staying.

"Oh, I've got to go back on Monday. I'm recording on Tuesday."

"What's the program?" I asked.

"It's a docudrama about the Bloomsbury set. I've got Laurel Makepeace as Virginia Woolf and Matthew Franklin as Lytton Strachey, so it's really quite an interesting production."

"It sounds marvelous," I said. "I'll look forward to hearing it. Your mother said you were hoping to have a word with Jo. Do you want her to talk about horses or something?"

Vicky smiled—a rather superior smile, reminiscent of her father. "*Not* horses," she said. "I'm contracted to do a series of arts programs. I don't know if you heard my program on Stravinsky; it had a very good notice in the *Spectator*. No, I'm planning something on the London postwar theater, and I want Jo to talk to me about her time at the Old Vic and at Stratford with James Carlyle and Jane Neville."

"It sounds fascinating."

"Well, it would be," Vicky said irritably, "if Jo would cooperate, but she's being very tiresome. She says it's all a long time ago and she can't remember anything interesting. It's nonsense. All actors love talking about their past triumphs, and she certainly had a lot of those."

"Perhaps," Simon put in gently, "she doesn't want to think about the past; well, *that* past, before she met Charlie, that is—especially now."

"I think Simon's right," I said. "The only time she wants to think about is her time with Charlie."

"Well, I think it's very selfish of her," Vicky said. "It wouldn't take long—just a couple of hours with a tape recorder; surely that's not too much to ask from a member of the family!"

Simon and I carefully avoided looking at each other.

"I'm sure you'll find someone else," he said. "Jane Neville's still around, isn't she?"

"Yes, and I've got something lined up with her, but it would have been so convenient to do Jo while I'm down here anyway."

"I think the rain has stopped now," I said, "so I'd better be getting along."

"We'll stay here a bit longer," Simon said. "We're keeping out of the way while Mother's preparing a special lunch—roast beef, Yorkshire, the lot. We have instructions to be back promptly at one thirty and I only hope we can do justice to it all!"

"It sounds lovely," I said, "and I'm sure it's giving her a lot of pleasure to do it."

A few weeks later I had a phone call from my cousin Hilda. She'd been at Bletchley Park during the war and now, she told me, there was to be a sort of reunion of some of the surviving members of the team.

"How lovely," I said. "You'll enjoy that."

"Oh, I can't possibly go."

"Why not?"

"For goodness' sake, Sheila, you of all people should know why I can't."

It was Tolly, of course. For most of her long life Hilda has steadfastly avoided animals, deriding those who are devoted to them. But in her fourth decade Hilda was obliged to take over the care of a small Siamese kitten and, on Hilda's part at least, it was love at first sight, and her life has revolved around him ever since.

"I can't possibly leave Tolly."

"No, of course not." I knew better than to suggest a cattery or a helpful neighbor. "Well, actually, I could do with a break," I said. "Shall I come?"

It was perfectly obvious to both of us that Hilda had rung me expecting precisely this response, though, of course, she'd never admit it.

"I wouldn't dream of it," she said. "You have such a busy life; you could hardly drop everything at a moment's notice."

"No, really," I said, "I'd love to have a few days in London—lots of things I want to do. It'll be a splendid opportunity to see people."

"I couldn't possibly let you."

"And I'd really like to look up a few things in the Senate House Library."

"Oh well, in that case . . ."

"When would you like me to come?"

"Thursday of next week," Hilda said briskly, abandoning any pretence of casualness. "It's a weekend meeting, but I'd need you here all day on Friday so that Tolly can get used to you while I'm still here."

"Honestly," Rosemary said, "you and your cousins—first it was Marjorie and now it's Hilda—using you as an invalid and cat sitter!"

"Oh, I don't mind. I enjoyed being up in the Lake District and it's ages since I had a trip to London. Mind you, the responsibility of looking after Tolly is a bit frightening. Anyway, you can't talk—all you do for Jilly and the children, not to mention your mother!"

"Oh, *don't* mention Mother," Rosemary said. "She's decided she needs a new winter coat—goodness knows why; she hardly ever goes out now. Luckily, Estelle lets me take several for Mother to choose from, but it means going back and forth umpteen times, and you know how sarcastic Estelle can be."

Estelle is the owner of our long-established dress shop (you wouldn't dare to call it a boutique), a formidable figure who has cowed many generations of customers. Only Rosemary's mother, Mrs. Dudley, has ever stood up to her and browbeaten her into submission.

"Oh, poor you, caught between the devil and the deep blue sea, though, of course, I wouldn't dream of saying which was which."

Rosemary laughed. "Oh well," she said. "Anyway, I expect you'd like me to have Tris while you're away?"

"Would you? That would be marvelous. He'll be much happier playing with your Alpha than getting overexcited about Thea's chickens. Foss, of course, simply ignores them."

"That's fine then. Drop him off on the way to the station."

"Bless you, now I can go away with a tranquil

mind—well, not tranquil exactly when I think of what a responsibility it's going to be looking after Tolly! Oh dear, I must dash. I'm collecting Alice from the stables and giving her her tea. Thea's got a dinner party this evening—a couple of Michael's colleagues—so she's up to her eyes."

It was a lovely afternoon at the stables and I stood peacefully leaning on the rails, looking down into the ring where Alice, under Peggy's watchful eye, was cantering cautiously round on Cracker. There was a clatter of hooves behind me and Jo came out of the yard on Tarquin. She waved to me and rode off. They certainly made a splendid picture: the superb horse with its confident rider moving easily across the fields in the late-afternoon sunshine.

"They're great together." Liz came up behind me, echoing my thoughts.

"He's a beautiful animal," I said, "but is he all right now? Safe to ride, I mean."

"He's pretty highly strung and it's fairly obvious that he hasn't been properly handled, but he's fine now with Jo and me. Actually, I think it's been good for Jo to work with him like that. She'd stopped going out much, with the rides and so forth, but she's out every day now on Tarquin."

"It seemed strange to me at first, how she could bear to keep him—after Charlie—but I do see now that it's been a good thing for her. That and working in the stables generally."

"Well, you know, it's her life and somehow

there's the connection with Charlie—we all feel that."

"You and Peggy have been wonderful, the way you've supported her," I said.

"Well," Liz spoke quietly, "the stables are my life too. I had a miserable childhood. My parents were divorced and I hated my stepfather and left home as soon as I could. I'd always been mad about horses and although I was only sixteen and pretty useless, they took me on and looked after me and taught me everything I know. Jo and Charlie have been my family." She stopped abruptly, as if she had said too much and, indeed, I'd never known her to talk about herself before. "I'd better get the jumps set up. I've got a class coming soon. Your Alice is doing very well. She's a natural."

"She's horse mad too," I said, and Liz smiled as she went down into the field to put up the apparatus.

I enjoyed being in London, though I do find that every time I go there it's changed and, usually, to my elderly mind, not for the better—change and decay, indeed. Hilda's little mews house in Holland Park, which she bought for a song just after the war, is now part of a very desirable area, and her neighbors, instead of the agreeable mix of all ages and classes they used to be, are now universally young and affluent. The little corner shop, dark and inconvenient, but friendly and a cheerful meeting place, is now a specialty cheese shop, and the newsagent next door is an exclusive boutique, which appears to sell only (unbelievably expensive) handbags.

Tolly greeted me amiably enough. Possibly he remembered me (as Hilda maintained), but he probably just recognized a born slave and was prepared to accept me as such.

"I've written out his daily schedule," Hilda said, presenting me with several closely printed sheets. "Meal times and so forth. He only has tinned food, organic, of course, once a day for breakfast and I like to rotate the various varieties, so I've put stickers with the appropriate day on each of the tins on his shelf in the larder. I've cooked the fish and chicken; it's in the fridge, and you just heat it up in the microwave. I usually do it for twenty seconds on high and then let it cool down a little naturally so it's *just* warm, which is how he likes it." She consulted the papers again. "Now, I let him out first thing and try to get him in after half an hour, and the same in the afternoon, if you happen to be in, but *never* after three thirty. He sleeps on my bed, of course, though while I'm away he may just come and sleep on yours for company." She handed me the papers. "Have a look through this while I go and make a cup of tea, and then if there's anything you want to ask me . . ."

Tolly jumped up onto the table beside me and sat looking smug. When I stroked his head he nipped my hand, not out of malice, you understand, but merely to indicate my place in the hierarchy.

Hilda came back with the tea tray, which she put down beside Tolly. He inspected the milk jug but, deciding it wasn't worth investigating fully, he jumped down and went upstairs.

"I'll be back on Tuesday," Hilda said, "just after lunch. My train gets in at two fifteen. I've left my telephone number beside the phone. It's my mobile number, so you will, of course, ring me if there's any sort of problem at *any* time. Now," she continued, pouring the tea, "how are the children? As you know, they came to see me a little while ago. Dear Michael and Thea, it was lovely to see them and I was most impressed with Alice, such a nice child. She was very good at playing with Tolly and he quite took to her."

Fortunately, it rained most of the time I was in London, so Tolly didn't want to go out and I was spared the agony of not being able to get him in. For myself, I went to several exhibitions and once to a matinee of a new play that had been greatly praised, but which I found dull and overwritten. I wondered idly how Jo would have fared in the theater of today and decided that she'd been wise to get out when she did.

For the sake of telling Hilda that I had, I spent the Monday afternoon in the Senate House Library, looking up some things I felt I might need for an article I'd been putting off writing. I'd just got back and was thinking I might indulge myself by going out to supper at the very trendy bistro nearby, when the phone rang. It was Rosemary.

"Hello," I said, surprised. "I thought you'd be

Hilda. She's been ringing up at least once a day since she left to check on Tolly's well-being."

"No, it's me." She sounded very subdued.

"What's the matter? Is something wrong? Is it the children?"

"No, no, they're fine," Rosemary said hastily, "and Tris too. It's just—just I thought you'd want to know. It's Jo; she's dead."

"Dead? What happened? Was it that horse?"

"Horse?"

"Tarquin, the one who killed Charlie. Did he throw her? I *knew* she should never have taken it on."

"No, nothing like that. She was electrocuted."

"*What?* How?"

"She always goes in last thing to switch on the electric fences—they leave them on at night. The switch is in the office. Apparently there was some sort of fault—I don't know the details—and she was electrocuted. Liz found her when she arrived for work."

"How awful for her, poor girl," I said, remembering the brief conversation I'd had with Liz just before I came away.

"Yes, it must have been terrible. But she kept her head and switched everything off at the mains, then tried to revive Jo. She couldn't, so she called an ambulance, but there was nothing they could do; it was too late."

"I can't believe it. First Charlie, now Jo—it's like some horrible curse on the place."

"Simon is dreadfully upset. You know how fond

he was of Jo, more than Esther really, though I suppose I shouldn't say so."

"I know," I agreed. "So what's happening?"

"Well, since it was some sort of accidental death I suppose there'll have to be an inquest. I must ask Roger."

"Have they closed the stables?"

"Well, they had to yesterday, when it happened, but Liz said that Jo would have wanted her to carry on, so she and Peggy are coping. I'm sure they're right."

"It's what Jo said when Charlie died," I remembered, "so I'm sure that *is* what she'd want."

"It's going to be hard work, running those stables with just the two of them," Rosemary said, "and it would probably cost more than they can afford to employ somebody. Simon's going to be up there every evening and at weekends, and, of course, all the young girls, like Delia, love helping out, but it's not a very satisfactory way to run a business."

"Oh, I'm sure they'll keep it going somehow," I said. "There's so much enthusiasm there."

But after Rosemary had rung off, I began to wonder just how they would manage and tried to think of various ways it could be done. After half an hour of fruitless thought I realized I'd been dwelling on that side of things to avoid thinking about Jo. It seemed inconceivable that she should be gone too, when we'd barely become accustomed to the idea of Charlie's death. And such a bizarre way to die—as Charlie's had been.

I didn't sleep much that night, turning facts and conjectures over and over in my mind. In the morning I felt thoroughly wretched, and my mood wasn't helped by Tolly who, taking advantage of the rain having stopped, went out straight after breakfast and didn't reappear until just before Hilda was due back. What with roaming the streets looking for him, going back and forth to the door hoping he might suddenly appear and wondering what on earth I'd say to Hilda if anything had happened to him, I was in a bad state when Tolly finally strolled in. I just had time to give him his fish before I heard the taxi.

After the first enthusiastic greeting (on Hilda's part; Tolly was distinctly offhand), I made a cup of tea and heard all about the reunion. It had obviously been a great success from Hilda's point of view since (according to her) all the others were in advanced stages of decrepitude (physical and mental).

"Elinor Bradshaw looked an absolute *wreck*. Her face has just caved in, a mass of wrinkles—quite extraordinary, considering how much time and trouble she used to devote to her appearance. Mavis Foster is hobbling about on two sticks and Bryan Adams's memory has practically gone. He simply didn't remember some of the procedures that used to be second nature to us all! Stone-deaf too and wouldn't wear a hearing aid."

I looked at Hilda, upright and healthy, in full possession of all her faculties, and thought how irritating she must have been to all her contemporaries gathered there. While she was having her second cup of tea I told her about Jo.

"What an unnecessary way to die," was her comment. "I remember her in *Twelfth Night*. She was the best Viola I have ever seen."

"So you see," I said, "I don't think I can stay until Friday. I really ought to get back tomorrow."

"Is there anything useful you can do for anyone at all by going back?" Hilda demanded.

"Well, no, but . . ."

"Then don't be ridiculous," she said firmly. "Stay. I have several things planned for us to do in the next few days."

And, of course, when Hilda is firm, there is no option but to obey.

Chapter Eleven

"I simply can't believe it," I said to Rosemary when she brought Tris home. "It's just too much to take in. First Charlie's accident, and now Jo's, both at the stables."

"I know, and both such unlikely things to happen."

"What exactly *did* happen to Jo?" I asked. "You said she was just switching on the electric fences?"

"Well, I don't really know the layout there," Rosemary said, "but the switch for the fences is in the office along with some other switches. Apparently there's a lot of separate wiring for them all—a regular tangle, Simon says. He said he did tell Jo, once, that he thought it was dangerous and that the whole place ought to be rewired. Anyway, as far as I can gather, there was a fault in the wiring for the fences and—well—when she switched it on, it killed her."

"And she must have lain there all night—how horrible."

"Yes, poor Liz was terribly upset, thinking that if she'd only found Jo earlier she might have been saved."

"Hilda said it was an unnecessary way to die," I said, "which I thought was unfeeling of her, but she's right; it *was* an avoidable accident, which somehow makes it even more tragic."

"I know. And Simon feels responsible in a way—he thinks he should have insisted on her getting it sorted out. But, really, I suppose she had so much on her mind that she simply put it to one side, as you do. Simon was busy just then—he's Gordon's executor—and then there was Esther. . . ."

"Of course, there's Gordon too. Good heavens— three deaths in one family, and in such a short space of time. It's like a Greek tragedy! Well, hardly that, but you know what I mean."

"It is extraordinary, and it all comes onto Simon's shoulders."

"How is Esther taking it—Jo's death, I mean?" I asked.

"She's upset, of course, but I think she's still trying to get used to Gordon being dead, so it hasn't really registered with her yet."

"I suppose we don't know yet when the funeral is to be?"

"Well, I suppose there'll have to be an inquest, so I don't think it'll be for a bit."

"No, I suppose not. Will Vicky come down from London? I wonder. She didn't for Charlie's funeral."

"Oh, she's here at the moment. She had to come down; something about her signature being needed for some documents. Apparently Gordon set up a complicated trust for Vicky and Simon—a way of avoiding death duties—and, of course, anything to do with money and Vicky's onto it like a shot. It was just before Jo died and I think Vicky was still hoping to get her to do something for that program of hers."

"Vicky can be very persistent, but I expect she was disappointed. Jo was really firm about not wanting to do it."

"Vicky's so like her father in some ways," Rosemary said, "self-centered and determined to get her own way, *and* the money thing—not a bit like Simon. I think he takes after Gordon's cousin Clive—you remember him?"

"Yes, I do, vaguely. He was much older than us, so we didn't have much to do with him, but I seem to remember he was rather nice."

"Mother always said that he wanted to marry Jo," Rosemary said, "and, when she turned him down—she was years younger than he—he went to Australia."

"To mend his broken heart?"

"Something like that. Not that he did, poor chap—he was drowned in a sailing accident in New South Wales."

I was just attempting to make sense of the notes I'd taken in the Senate House Library, when Michael turned up with some eggs.

"Oh, lovely, now I can have a Spanish omelet for supper," I said. "Are the hens laying still? They tend to fall off a bit at this time of the year, don't they? Hang on while I turn off my computer and I'll come and make you a cup of tea."

Michael followed me into the study and looked disapprovingly at my electric fire.

"That's dangerous," he said.

"What, the fire? It was really quite cold today, but I didn't want to put all the heating on."

"No, not the fire itself, but you really oughtn't to have that trailing lead on it."

"I wanted it near me to keep my feet warm. My circulation's really miserable these days."

"Well, it's not safe like that," Michael said firmly.

"I suppose you're right," I agreed. "And after poor Jo—well it's a lesson to us all to be more careful with electrical things."

"What you really need," Michael went on, "is a point on the other side of your desk. If you had it there it would be away from the plugs and things for your computer."

"Yes, well, I'll have to see to it."

"As a matter of fact, Steve is doing some wiring for us at the moment."

"Oh," I said, "whereabouts?"

"It's outside lighting to help us see to the chickens when it gets dark early and we hope, if we leave it on, it might discourage the foxes."

"What a good idea!"

"Anyway," Michael said, reverting to his theme, "you really must have this seen to. I'll get Steve to give you a ring to say when he can come."

*   *   *

I was in the kitchen at Brunswick Lodge unpacking the cakes I'd brought for the Wednesday coffee morning, when Anthea appeared.

"Oh good," she said, "you're back. You always seem to be away on holiday these days."

I considered explaining to Anthea that they hadn't been holidays exactly, but I refrained, partly because it would take too long, but mostly because I knew she wouldn't listen anyway.

"I wanted to have a word," Anthea went on. "I'm rallying all the support I can get."

"Oh," I said warily.

"It's this dreadful business of poor Jo Hamilton. I was really shocked when I heard. But it's a lesson to us all. So I thought about our electrical wiring here."

"It's all right, isn't it?" I asked. "Surely we had someone in a few months ago to put some more points in."

"Yes, we did," Anthea said impatiently, "but that's not what I mean. This is an old house and I think the whole system needs a thorough overhaul."

"Well, I suppose it might. . . ."

"It's not just the helpers," she said. "We do hold events here, so members of the public are at risk too."

"I think 'at risk' is going a bit far," I said.

"Health and Safety," Anthea said impressively. "We might be liable for all sorts of things."

"But we have insurance, don't we?"

"Oh, I'm sure that doesn't count if it's a government thing. But what's important," she repeated, "is to have the whole system overhauled."

"I'm sure it's not necessary," I said feebly, knowing from bitter experience that if Anthea had an idea in her head it was virtually impossible to dislodge it. "Besides," I added, "it would cost the earth. We simply don't have the funds."

She smiled patronizingly. "That's where my scheme comes in."

"Oh?"

It's perfectly simple. We will apply for lottery money."

"But we'd never get *that*," I said. "It's for big projects—stately homes, Victorian piers, that sort of thing."

"Not a bit of it. I saw on the television the other day some villagers got it for extending their village hall. Now if *they* can get it to put up an extension to a wooden hut, then Brunswick Lodge, a historic house, certainly deserves it."

"Well, I suppose. . . ."

"I haven't got all the information yet. I thought I would sound out public opinion first."

That, of course, was sheer sophistry, since, in my long experience, Anthea has never been known to consider any opinion other than her own.

"Well," I said cautiously, "I suppose it wouldn't hurt to give it a try."

"The thing is," Anthea said, "I believe we would have to raise a proportion of the money ourselves."

"What sort of proportion?"

"Oh, I don't know," she said impatiently. "That's a minor point. The thing is to get the ball rolling as soon as possible."

"Well yes, if you think . . ."

"Good. I've spoken to all the trustees and most of the committee—I'd have come to you before if you hadn't been away—and they all think it's a marvelous idea."

"I'm sure they do," I said. And, indeed, I knew they would all be delighted to have extra funds if someone else did the work, though they would reserve the right to criticize and complain at every stage of the proceedings.

"So I'll write away and get all the forms and things. It really is important that we get something done about that wiring. Poor Esther, *another* death in the family; she must be dreadfully upset. She didn't send the ginger cake she promised for the bring and buy sale, but, of course, I quite understood."

Having a son who shoots and plays cricket is marvelous; it opens up a whole range of people who engage in useful activities. Michael's mates now include doctors, dentists, plumbers, carpenters, electricians, computer wizards, and (should you need them) gamekeepers and slaughterhouse workers—just to give a general cross section—who will all turn up and *do* things for you when you need them. Michael, on his part, provides general legal advice as part of the give-and-take. Steve is one of the cricketing fraternity (useful medium-pace bowler who can bat a bit) and he duly turned up the following day.

"I've got a job on at Porlock," he said, accepting a cup of tea and a biscuit, "so I thought I'd drop in on my way and see what the problem is."

"Just another point, really," I said, "but, actually, what I'd really like is for you to move most of the points higher up. I find bending right down a bit of a problem now. And with the angle they're at, I can get the plugs in all right, but I find pulling them *out* quite difficult."

"No problem, Mrs. M. I can put battens in at waist height if you like."

"That's marvelous. And I do feel now that I ought to pull plugs out at night, just to be sure, after what happened to poor Jo Hamilton. That really was a terrible thing, an accident that should never have happened."

Steve shook his head. "I'm not so sure," he said.

"What do you mean, not sure?"

"Well, I don't know if I should be telling you this, but when it happened, Bob Morris, who's in charge—he's an inspector now; done very well—anyway, he asked me to have a look at the wiring up there at the stables. Bob used to play for Taviscombe, you remember, a couple of seasons ago—wicketkeeper, a really safe pair of hands—and we're mates, so it was sort of unofficial, if you know what I mean." I nodded. "Well, anyhow, I went up there and you wouldn't *believe* the state of that wiring." I made a murmur of horror. "What you might call real spaghetti—wires all tangled up; you wouldn't credit it!"

He paused for me to take in the enormity of what he was saying.

"Really?" I said.

He leaned forward as if to emphasize the confidential nature of what he was about to say. "When I'd sorted that lot out, guess what I found?" I shook my head. "That lead—the one for the electric fences—it was frayed all right; easy to see how it could have shorted and killed someone. But" he paused to give the full effect—"*but*, that fraying was never just ordinary wear and tear. Oh, it might have looked like it to a layman's eye, as they say, but I could tell. It had been frayed deliberately!"

"Are you sure?" I asked.

"As sure as I'm sitting here. Deliberately. If you knew what you were looking for, you could just see the marks where someone had been at it with a knife."

"But that's terrible."

"Exactly, that's what Bob Morris said to me when I told him. 'That's terrible, Steve,' he said. 'That means this wasn't an accidental death at all. This could be murder.' He said, 'Would you stand up in court and say that lead had been tampered with?' and I said 'Yes, I take my oath it had.'"

"But it's impossible. Who on earth would want to kill Jo? Everyone loved her!"

Steve shook his head. "Well, you never know, do you. Like they say, human nature's a terrible thing. Well, I must be off. Mrs. Henderson'll be wonder-

ing what's become of me. I'll give you a ring sometime next week about those points."

When he'd gone I sat for quite a while trying to
take in the implications of what he'd said. It had
been bad enough to face the fact that Jo was dead
without this terrible new possibility. I could think
of no one (apart from Charlie) who was so well
liked, no one less likely to be—I could hardly bring
myself the even think the word—murdered. But
Steve was a good electrician, very experienced and
unlikely to make a mistake, and certainly not in a
situation like this.

Tris, who'd been sitting quietly at my feet,
began to make little whining noises, which meant
that he wanted to go out. Foss, suddenly material-
izing beside him, jumped up onto the table, to the
imminent danger of the tea things, making his own
vocal demands. I got up slowly and took the tray
over to the sink and let the animals out into the
garden. On an impulse I phoned Thea.

"Steve's just been here to see about the points
for me," I said.

"Oh good, Michael said he'd rung him. He's
very good. He did a marvelous job for us with that
outdoor light. It's made such a difference."

"Yes, I'm sure it has. Actually, when he was here
he said something about Jo's accident at the stables." I told her what Steve had told me about the
wiring. "And now Bob Morris thinks Jo was—was
killed deliberately."

"I don't believe it," Thea said. "Not Jo—who'd
want to kill her? It's ridiculous."

"I know, but Steve was absolutely positive and there's no way he'd have said anything if it wasn't true."

"No, I suppose not, but it's an awful thought. I wonder what's happening. You know Bob Morris, don't you? Could you ask him?"

"I'm not quite sure how I could approach him, but I'll think about it. Roger would be the one to ask, of course, but his work is in Taunton now."

But, as it happened, I ran into Roger quite by chance early on Sunday morning, both of us dog walking on the beach.

"Hallo," he said, looking up at the threatening sky. "I thought I might be the only one out today, but I know the weather doesn't normally put you off."

"Oh, Tris loves the beach and it's one of the few places I can let him run free. Anyway, it's always a pleasure to walk here when there's virtually no one about." We stood silently for a moment looking at the empty beach and the sea until I said, "Actually, I'm so glad I saw you. I wondered if you knew what's happening about Jo's death."

Roger smiled. "I thought you might ask me that. Well, as you know, I've got nothing to do with the case. Bob Morris is in charge for the moment. They might send CID down if they think it's necessary, but we've got a lot of faith in having the local man investigating—and, anyway, there's the usual manpower shortage. No, Bob's a good chap and will do a thorough job."

"I did hear," I said tentatively, "that it's possible

it might not have been an accident. Something about the wiring . . ."

"Now, how did you hear about that?" Roger said, looking at me quizzically. "No, don't tell me—it's probably something I shouldn't know. Yes, there was a query about that, so, of course, we sent in forensics to have a special look at it and they agreed that it might have been tampered with."

"So, what then? Is it murder?"

"For the moment it's being classified as suspicious death, but it depends how the inquiries go if it needs to be upgraded to murder."

"But Roger, you knew Jo. Who would want to kill her? No one would want her dead!"

He shook his head. "I know, it does sound unlikely, but I'm afraid one thing experience has taught me is that in the case of murder, no matter how improbable it seems, there is always someone who wanted the victim dead."

Chapter Twelve

Life goes on. It was half term and Alice had been promised a couple of rides. I said I'd take her for the second one.

"Gran," Alice said as we drove to the stables, "Mummy said Jo's died and that's why she wasn't there on Monday."

"I'm afraid so, darling."

"Like Charlie died?"

"Yes, like Charlie."

"Will she be with Charlie now?"

"I expect so, darling."

"Liz was very sad on Monday. She'd been crying. I expect she loved Jo very much."

When I'd handed Alice over to Peggy and went to pay for her ride, I found the door of the office locked and Liz in the tack room. She was in tears. I made a move as if to go away, but she motioned me to come back.

"No, please," she said. "I'm sorry. Don't go away."

"Poor Liz," I said, "it must be very hard for you."

She felt for a crumpled tissue in her shirt pocket

and wiped her eyes. "It's been awful," she said, "but I was just beginning to come to terms with it when I got the news."

"What news?"

"About Jo's will and—," She broke off. "And she's left me the house and a share in the stables." The tears came again. "I never thought—it's too much—I don't want any of that. I just want her back."

"I'm sure you do," I said gently, "but you must do your best to carry on for her and remember how much she must have thought of you to leave you things she cared about so much."

She nodded. "I know, but I just can't help . . ."

"I know."

"But the house—it should have gone to Simon. He was her family."

"She obviously thought of you as family too. And, really, she knew that Simon couldn't leave his mother and move in here, not now his father is dead."

"No, but. . ."

"And," I continued, "she knew someone had to live here, on the premises, to look after things, day or night, and she knew she could trust you to do that."

"Yes, of course, you're right." Liz gave herself a little shake (a characteristic gesture) and mopped her eyes again. "That's what she wanted me to do and I mustn't let her down."

"I'm sure Simon feels the same."

"Yes, I think he does. He said we must do what

she wanted. He was very kind. He's been wonderful ever since—you know. Up here every spare minute he has from his job. We couldn't have managed without him. He says we can't afford to hire anyone else and that's all right; I'm sure we can manage. Peggy's been great, working all hours for no extra money."

"Are you still busy?"

"Most of our regulars still come, but a few people have canceled. I suppose they think it's not safe or something."

"Things will sort themselves out."

"That's what Simon says. He says we must have a proper meeting soon, the three of us, to plan for the future, but—well, we've been so busy."

"I'm sure Simon will manage things; he's very methodical."

"Yes, he's brilliant."

I was silent for a moment. Then I asked, "Have the police finished here now?"

"I think so. Inspector Morris came at the beginning—you know—and asked me how I found Jo and that sort of thing. He came several times to look at things in the office. Then a couple of people came back with him and they examined it as well, something to do with the wiring. Inspector Morris wanted to know if anyone had checked the wiring or the switch lately, but I couldn't tell him. I suppose they might have done, but you know how it is here; we're in and out all the time and don't take much notice of things." She stopped suddenly. "If only we *had* noticed something wrong, Jo wouldn't have died—that's awful!"

"The office is locked now?"

"Yes, Inspector Morris asked us to keep it locked. Until he'd finished making inquiries, he said. Anyway," she went on, "I don't think any of us want to use it now."

There was a knock on the door and a woman and a young girl came in to make a booking, so I put the money for Alice's ride on the shelf that Liz was using for a desk and went outside. Peggy was calling out instructions to the children riding round the ring, just as Jo used to do.

"Sit deep in the saddle, Jemma. Keep your contact, Poppy. Your reins are like washing lines! Fiona, squeeze; don't *kick*. Heels *down*, Alice— you're not keeping your balance—that's better."

It all seemed so timeless, somehow, as if, any moment, Charlie would come limping out of the stable block and Jo would lead Tarquin out into the sunshine. They'd seemed so secure, happy in their own little world; hard to believe that it and they had gone forever. After a while Peggy led the children back out of the ring; Alice dismounted and led Cracker over to where I was standing.

"Gran, Peggy said I can go in with Fiona and help with the tack."

I looked at Peggy, who nodded. "All right," I said, "but not too long, because Mummy will be expecting us back for tea."

The children went off into the stable yard and I turned to Peggy.

"It must be difficult, just the two of you doing everything," I said.

She shrugged. "We manage," she said. "A lot of the kids like helping and they're pretty useful, and Simon comes in every day. But we miss Jo, not just for the stable work, but in lots of ways—well, you can imagine."

"Of course. I think you're all doing wonderfully."

"It's hit Liz hardest. I've got my own family, but Jo and Charlie were her family and you can see she's lost without them."

"I gather the police haven't finished with the office yet," I said tentatively.

"No. Inspector Morris—He's a friend of my uncle Chris; they both used to be on the skittles team for the Stag's Head out at Roadwater—he says the inquiry is ongoing, whatever that means. I suppose they're still trying to find out what happened. He's been back and forth several times—well, it was a dreadful thing to happen."

"Indeed it was and I'm sure he wants to get to the bottom of it. Liz didn't seem to know much about how things are going."

"She's still in a state. If you think about it, she found Charlie and then she was the one to find poor Jo. It's no wonder it's all got to her. She gets through the work—works all the hours God sends, but it's all about the horses and the stables. I don't think she's taken in half of what's happening."

"Poor girl. She's very lucky to have you to support her."

"We all support each other, the kids as well, because it's what Jo and Charlie would want."

"I'm sure it is," I agreed.

We both stood for a while in silence, looking out across the fields to where a small group of riders were emerging from the woods beyond.

"There's the four o'clock ride," Peggy said. "I'd better go and open the gates for them."

I watched while they came in and to my surprise I saw that one of the riders was Vicky. When they got back into the yard, Vicky dismounted and handed the reins to Peggy with a cursory word of thanks and turned to me.

"I didn't expect to see you here, Sheila. Are you *still* riding?"

I wasn't terribly keen on the "still," but I smiled and explained that I was collecting Alice.

"I thought I'd get back in the saddle," she said, "though I know I'll be hellish stiff tomorrow. Still, now it's all in the family, it's free! Trust Simon to get all this—but he always was Jo's favorite."

"He's putting in a lot of work," I said repressively. "He's up here all hours."

"Well, he knows he's got to keep the business going if he wants to get anything for it."

"Oh no, I'm sure he wouldn't dream of selling it."

"Maybe you're right. Daddy always said that for an accountant, he had absolutely no business sense."

"How long are you down here for?" I asked.

"Just until the weekend. I've got a lot on my

plate with this program and now that Jo's gone, I'll have to find someone else to cover that period."

"But she didn't agree, did she? I thought she had reservations about it."

"I was working on her," Vicky said. "Actually, I came up here to see her the day before she died and I think she was beginning to change her mind. Pity."

"It was a tragic accident," I said, "absolutely tragic."

"Yes, terrible," she said absently, "but I would have thought it was perfectly obvious how it happened—that whole office was chaotic—so I can't see why the police are questioning everybody like this."

"Are they?"

"Simon, of course, because he was always up here, but why should they want to talk to me? I don't know anything about the wiring, or whatever it was. And coming and bothering Mother like that! I mean, she's been right out of it since Daddy died, and I don't know if she's really taken in what's happened to Jo. She's been very upset."

"Poor Esther, I'm so sorry," I said, "but I suppose they do have to make inquiries where there are unusual circumstances."

"Unusual?" Vicky said sharply. "It was an accident."

"Yes, but there has to be an inquest."

"A lot of nonsense. Well, I hope they don't expect me to stay down here for that. I'm up to my eyes at the moment. Not only this theater program, but I've scheduled one about women Victorian novelists. There's been a lot of interest ever since that TV *Jane Eyre*, and what was that Gaskell one?"

"*North and South.*"

"That's it." She eyed me speculatively. "You know about these people—you've written books and stuff about them. How would you like to take part in the program?"

"Oh, I don't think so," I said firmly. "It's not my sort of thing at all."

"It would be good for the sales of your books," Vicky said, "all good publicity."

"My books are mostly bought by libraries, so I don't think. . ."

"Well, give it some thought. I wouldn't be able to get down here to record anything, but you could easily go to the Bristol studios."

"No, really," I said, starting to move away. "I'd better go and retrieve Alice or she'll be here all night."

Michael got back just as I'd finished having tea with Thea and Alice and saw me out to my car.

"When did you last check the oil and tires?" he asked.

"I don't know—a while back."

"Give me the keys. I'll do it for you now."

"Thank you, darling. I would be grateful. I rather wanted to have a word with you," I went on as he opened the bonnet, "that's if it isn't all still confidential."

"All what?"

"About Jo's will. I had a chat with Liz today and she told me that Jo had left her the house and a share in the stables."

"Yes, that's right. Everything else goes to Simon—the rest of the share of the stables and all the land."

"Nothing to Esther or Vicky?"

"No. Jo never did get on with Vicky and I suppose she thought Esther would be looked after by Gordon. She made a new will quite recently, just after Charlie died. But no surprises really."

"Liz was surprised about the house, and a bit upset."

"Why on earth was she upset?"

"Well, she felt she shouldn't have had it. She said it was too much and Simon ought to have had everything—that sort of thing. She was very emotional."

Michael wiped the dipstick on a tissue I handed him and shut the bonnet. "I'll never understand women," he said. "Why can't they ever accept things as they are instead of agonizing over them!"

"Well, poor Liz is in a bit of a state just now. I mean, Charlie gone and then Jo, and, although *she'd* thought of them as her family, the fact that they weren't really made her feel the house should have gone to Jo's actual relations."

"It wouldn't have been in the will if Jo hadn't wanted her to have it." He opened the boot and took out the foot pump.

"I know, and that's what I told her, of course, but I suppose people don't think logically at times like this. And it won't be any easier if Bob Morris decides to make it a murder inquiry."

"Yes, Thea told me what Steve said about the wiring. But the thought that anyone would want to murder Jo is, well, ridiculous."

"That's what I thought, but Roger says they're treating it as a suspicious death, so *someone* must think it's a possibility."

"I still think it's rubbish. This front tire's a bit down. I'll just pump it up."

When I got back I let the animals out into the garden to give myself a little peace to get my supper. I'd eaten rather too much of Thea's gorgeous Victoria sponge to be really hungry and I'd just decided that a plain boiled egg was all I wanted, when the phone rang. It was Rosemary.

"Sorry to be the bearer of bad tidings," she said, "but Mother asked—no *told*—me to ask you to go to tea there next Friday."

I laughed. "I promise not to shoot the messenger," I said, "and of course I'd love to go to tea. I've been feeling a bit guilty about not having seen her for a long time. Has she got over that nasty cold?"

"It did pull her down quite a bit, but she won a great battle with Dr. Macdonald and that set her up wonderfully."

"Battle?"

"Yes, she said she wanted an antibiotic and he said, quite rightly, that they don't do anything for colds."

"But?"

"But Mother did the usual—weak chest, threat of pleurisy if not pneumonia, appalling state of the Health Service, so much for patient choice, criminal lack of government spending on the elderly, et cetera, et cetera."

"So?"

"So, of course, he gave her the mildest possible tablets and she made a splendid recovery, which she, of course, attributed to the antibiotic, but was really her triumph over him!"

I laughed. "She's an example to us all! I'll look forward to hearing all about it next Friday."

"I think," Rosemary said, "she wants to question you about Jo."

"What has she heard?"

"Something about the wiring and it not being an accident."

"How on earth did she hear about that?" I asked.

"You know Mother's system of intelligence gathering. But really, Sheila, is it true? Is there some doubt about it?"

"I think so; no, I'm sure. Steve Webber—you know, the electrician— told me he thought the wire in the office had been cut deliberately, and he's very reliable. I mean, he wouldn't have said anything unless he was certain. And I had a word with Roger when I met him dog walking and he said they were treating it as a suspicious death."

"I can't imagine anyone wanting Jo dead," Rosemary said.

"That's what we all feel," I said, "but, if what

Steve says is true—and Roger said the forensic people have checked as well—then I suppose we simply have to consider the possibility, however unlikely."

Chapter Thirteen

I was flicking through the program pages of the *Radio Times* when I saw that one of the satellite stations was doing a rerun of the *Inspector Ivor* series, with my old friend David Beaumont. David's a childhood friend who became an actor and is now running a sort of Shakespeare institute in Stratford-upon-Avon. We've always stayed in touch, and sometimes I go and stay with him in his lovely little cottage opposite the Memorial Theatre to catch up on the gossip. On an impulse I rang him.

"Hello, darling," the deep, familiar voice greeted me. "I was just thinking about you. Well, you and poor Jo Howard. I heard it on the news and there was a nice obit in the *Guardian*. What a ghastly thing to happen. You must all have been devastated."

"We were. Still are, really. You played with her, didn't you?" I said, giving him the cue that would, I knew, produce the anecdotes I wanted.

"Yes, of course I did, my first proper part: Osric in the Carlyle *Hamlet*, here at Stratford. Her Ophelia was quite wonderful—technically perfect with that little extra something, *so* rare to combine the two. Ellen could, of course, but hardly anybody now—perhaps Vanessa. She was just coming to that point—enough experience, all the big roles, but hadn't lost the freshness—when she could do no wrong. Everything she touched was magic. The critics *adored* her and her name could sell any production."

"Was that the only time you played with her?"

"Well, yes, she gave it all up, absolutely mad. None of us could believe it at the time."

"When she married Charlie Hamilton?"

"Oh no, before that."

"Really?"

"About a year before."

"Do you know why?"

There was a pause at the other end. "Well, darling, there *were* rumors."

"Rumors?"

"About her and John Carlyle."

"Oh?"

"Just greenroom gossip. You know what it's like with a permanent company. Jane wasn't around; she was abroad filming. Do you remember her, Jane Neville? I believe she's practically gaga now, living at Denville Hall anyway. She had absolutely *scathing* notices for her Lady Macbeth, even worse than Tynan on Vivien Leigh, total madness, of course. I mean, she was splendid in *School for Scandal* and a lovely Gwendolen in *The Importance*. She did that mannered stuff very well, but to think she could play Shakespeare, let alone Lady

Macbeth . . . Well, think of Marie Tempest playing Goneril!"

"So did they?" I asked, trying to bring him back to the point. "Have an affair—Jo and John Carlyle?"

"Oh yes."

"But surely that wasn't enough to make her give up acting!"

"It was a bit more than that, though I believe Jane had her suspicions. John wasn't the best of husbands, and she did all she could to wreck Jo's career. Jane had a lot of influence. Her father, Arthur Neville, was in management, you see."

"So what was it? You said it was a bit more than the affair."

Another pause. "Well, they're all dead or as good as, so I suppose it won't matter if I tell you. It was after a performance. I found John had left his watch in the greenroom. It was a *very* expensive one— given him by Jane and very lovingly inscribed—so I thought I'd better take it to him in his dressing room. The door was a bit ajar and I heard voices, so I was about to go away, but then I heard Jo's voice. She sounded absolutely distraught. I knew I *ought* to go away. It was unforgivable to listen, but, well, I was young and curious, so I stayed where I was."

"And?"

"I heard John telling her to control herself—his voice was really unpleasant—and after a while she was quiet. Then he said, quite coldly, 'I've told you, you'll have to get rid of it.' He could really be a swine if something upset him. A lot of directors found him very difficult. I know for a fact that after that production of *Winter's Tale*, Guthrie swore he'd never work with him again."

"So what happened? What did Jo say?"

"I couldn't hear her words. Her voice was very muffled as if she was crying, but then I heard him say, 'There's no other way. You know that; you're not a fool. I know of a clinic and I'll pay for it, so if you're sensible and discreet, no one need ever find out. You know it makes sense, for both our careers.' His voice was softer then. He was obviously trying to persuade her—he *could* be very persuasive when he wanted."

"So what did she say?"

"I don't know. I heard someone coming. so I had to go, but it was perfectly obvious what was going on."

"You mean she was pregnant and he wanted her to get rid of it?"

"What else?"

"How horrible."

"Typical though. He was always tremendously ambitious and it was just coming up to crunch time for the National Theatre. He thought he had a chance there and so, of course, he didn't want any sort of scandal. Still," David said with some satisfaction, "I'm glad to say that Larry beat him to it and got the job."

"Yes, I see. So did she, I wonder?"

"Did she what?"

"Did Jo have an abortion? It wasn't easy in those days."

"I don't know. After *Hamlet* I went to the Birmingham Rep—really very lucky. The Dauphin in *St. Joan* and Konstantin in *The Seagull*—we got some marvelous notices, even in the national press, and I made some really good contacts. So I rather lost touch and, as far as I can remember, the gossip never really amounted to anything in the end."

"But she still gave up the theater? A year before she married Charlie?"

"Round about a year. So, it did occur to me that perhaps she *did* have the baby."

"And put it up for adoption? No, that's not like Jo!"

"Well, as you rightly said, darling, things were very different then."

"I suppose so. . . ."

"Well, it was all a long time ago," David said, "so we'll never know now. But what I *do* want to know is when are you coming to stay? It's a good time of year. The main *swarms* of Japanese with cameras and French schoolchildren with their horrid backpacks have gone and I've got some gorgeous new exhibits to show you. A dear old soul in Warwick left us some absolutely marvelous set designs for the Beerbohm Tree *Dream* and a couple of scripts—real treasures."

"I'd love to come, David. I'm a bit tied up just now, but the minute I'm free I'll give you a ring. It'll be something to look forward to."

When I put the phone down I sat for a while trying to take in what David had told me. Marjorie's description of Jo and John Carlyle in the nunnery scene came into my mind. The animosity must have been very strong to have come over like that on stage.

Poor Jo. My heart ached for her. As David said, things were very different in those days. It was a miserable business, whether the illegal operation was done by a backstreet abortionist or in an expensive clinic where money changed hands and no questions were asked. And keeping an illegitimate child wasn't easy. The social stigma was immense. It must have often seemed easier to bear the pain of having the baby adopted than to face the condemnation of society and, even more, the stigma that would be attached to your child. The Jo I knew was very strong, but even she might have finally decided she couldn't cope, especially if she intended to carry on with her career—though she never did. It was very puzzling, but, as David said, it was all a long time ago and we'd probably never know now what had happened. Still, there was a nagging feeling at the back of my mind that it was just possible that Jo's child, now grown up, could exist and might one day have wanted to find his, or her, real mother.

The next day Steve came to change my electricity points.

"Well, I've put that new one in where you needed it and I've moved all the others up to make it easier for you," he said. "There's not a lot of making good—a bit of plastic wood and a lick of paint is all it needs. You'd better come and see if they're what you wanted."

I made a tour of the points with him, making, as one does, appreciative and admiring comments at each one.

"That's splendid," I said when we had finally finished, "just what I wanted; it'll make life *so* much easier! Now, do come and have a cup of tea. You'll need one after all that hard work!"

As I poured the tea and cut some slices of fruit cake, Steve said, "Funny thing about that inquest, wasn't it?"

"Inquest? What inquest?" I asked.

"For poor Mrs. Hamilton."

"Really—have they held it, then?"

"Last Friday."

"I'd no idea—I hadn't heard. I suppose it'll be in this week's *Free Press*. What happened?"

"Well," Steve said, stirring his tea vigorously, "you know what I said about that wiring, and how I told Bob Morris? So, I naturally thought I'd be called to say what I'd found." He added another spoonful of sugar to his tea and stirred it again. "But not a bit of it!"

"Really?"

"No. Bob goes and gets in the what-you-call-them—the *forensic* people to look at it again and they say it could have been an accident after all."

"But you said the wire had been cut."

"And I still say that's what it looked like to me— and I've been twenty years in the trade." He took a large bite of fruit cake. "It seems," he said, his sarcastic tone slightly muffled by a mouthful of crumbs, "it *seems* that there was a heavy, metal cash box they used to keep on that bench where the wiring and the switches were, and they said the sharp edge of that could have cut the wire."

"I suppose it might have done," I said. "It's just possible."

"Possible, perhaps," Steve said scornfully, "but is it likely? I ask you!"

"Well. . ."

"Any road, that's what *they* said, so I wasn't called to say what I thought, and the coroner, Major Barrington, that silly old fool, said it was accidental death."

"I see."

"But I saw what I saw, whatever they may say, and you can take it from me, Mrs. M, we haven't heard the last of it."

After he'd gone and while I was washing up and putting away the cake tin, my immediate feeling was one of relief. Of course it had been an accident, another tragic accident, just like Charlie's had been. Of course no one could possibly have wanted to kill Jo. Like everyone said, the whole idea was ridiculous. We could put away the feelings of distress and anxiety all the speculation had aroused and simply mourn the loss of a good friend.

Foss, who'd been banished outside to prevent him from taking part in Steve's activities, suddenly appeared at the window, demanding to be let in. I opened the door and took down a tin of cat food.

Tris, who was fast asleep in his basket, woke up instantly at the sound of a saucer being put down and, with a short, sharp bark, claimed his equal rights. As I shook the dog biscuits into his bowl I felt as if a load had been lifted from my mind.

Later, when I set off to collect Alice, I felt more cheerful about going to the stables than I had ever since Jo's death. When I got there I was surprised to see Roger, leaning on the fence leading down to the ring.

"Hello," I said. "Fancy seeing you here."

He smiled. "I've been detailed to collect my daughter," he said. "How about you?"

"I'm collecting Alice—grandmother's privilege. Actually," I went on, "for a moment, when I saw you here, I wondered if it was something to do with Jo's death."

"No, that's all done and dusted. The coroner's verdict was accidental death."

"So I gather. But I thought you told me that the forensic people thought the wiring might have been tampered with."

"So they did, but then they discovered that a heavy, metal cash box had often been dumped down on some of the wiring—people really are so careless—and that could easily have caused the cut. After that there was no reason to suspect foul play—especially against someone like Jo!"

"I'm so glad," I said. "It gave me a horrible feeling to think that anyone might have wanted to harm her. I'm sure Simon and Liz are so relieved.

They've got enough to worry about, running this place."

"They certainly have. I wouldn't like to have to cope with all those teenage girls."

I smiled. "Is Delia giving you a hard time?"

"Let's just say that Jilly and I have been thinking quite seriously about boarding school!"

"You don't mean it."

"No, I know it's only what our Mrs. Mac calls a 'phrase' she's going through and she'll come out the other end our own sweet daughter, but it's hard to live with. Alex is so much easier."

"Ah, just you wait until Alex is seventeen. That I *do* know about! Motor bikes," I said darkly, "and things like that."

The riders had come back while we were talking and Delia walked over, deep in conversation with Alice. Well, not conversation exactly, more like a monologue, which Alice was listening to with rapt attention.

"So you see," Delia was saying, "that's why it's easiest to slow your pony down with half halts—pull and let loose."

She graciously informed me that Alice was doing nicely and if she remembered to sit deeper in the saddle, she'd do very well. When she saw her father, however, she said, "Daddy, how *could* you come out in that *terrible* jacket!" and scrambled quickly into the car before anyone could associate her with such a dreadful sartorial mistake.

Roger pulled a face, waved to me and drove away.

Alice was tugging at my sleeve. "Gran, can I just go and help Peggy with the feed buckets? She said I could."

"Yes, all right, but don't be long."

"That's good. We need all the free labor we can get." Simon had come up behind me. "Thank heaven for little girls. I'm not sure we could function without them!"

"Well," I said, smiling, "it does appear to be mutually beneficial. Seriously though, how's it going?"

He shrugged. "I think we can manage to keep going, if we can get a few more liveries and don't lose any more clients."

"Liz said some of them have canceled."

"Only to be expected, I suppose—two fatal accidents, bound to put people off. But most people have been very loyal."

"I'm sure they want you to succeed, for Jo's sake," I said. "Actually, Simon, I haven't had a proper chance to tell you how very sorry I am about it all. I know how close you were to her and how badly you must miss her. And I'm so glad all this business with the police has been sorted out. That must have been so painful for you."

"Yes," he said, "it was difficult."

"Do you have a date for the funeral?"

"It's not quite settled yet. We've only just had permission to. . ." He had difficulty in finishing the sentence.

"Yes, of course," I said quickly. "I'm sure a lot of people will want to come. She was greatly loved."

"Yes."

"I think," I said, "I'd better go and sort out Alice. I'm sure she'd *sleep* here if she could!"

As I went into the stable yard I felt worried about Simon. He looked absolutely exhausted and was obviously in a highly emotional state. Given his burden of the stables as well as his own demanding job, not to mention looking after his mother following his father's death, I suppose it wasn't surprising. But I still felt there was something else preying on his mind.

I prized a reluctant Alice away from the delights of the hay nets and got her into the car.

I was driving down the track away from the stables when I had to pull over onto the grass to let a large Mitsubishi four-by-four go by. As the driver raised his hand to thank me, I saw that it was Dan Webster.

Chapter Fourteen

I like to take flowers to Mrs. Dudley when I visit her, but, since she has very definite views on the matter, it's always difficult to know *which* flowers. Not roses or carnations (unnatural nowadays, no scent), not lilies or chrysanthemums (funeral flowers), certainly not geberas (vulgar). Fortunately, I found some rather nice, properly scented freesias that I hoped might be acceptable.

"Freesias, how very nice," she said approvingly, and I breathed a sigh of relief. "Give them to Elsie and tell her to put them in the *tall* cut-glass vase."

I made my way into the kitchen and handed the flowers over to Elsie, who has been with Mrs. Dudley for as long as I can remember, remains cheerful at all times and is, thank goodness, impervious to her moods and general irascibility.

"How is she," I asked, "after that nasty cold?"

"A bit pulled down," Elsie said as she filled the required vase with water and arranged the flowers, "but she's picking up nicely, and Dr. Macdonald is very pleased with her. Of course, she does miss having her little lunch parties, but it really was getting to be too much for her."

"She's still amazing for her age," I said.

"There." Elsie handed me the vase. "If you'd take that in, I'll bring the tea. The kettle's just on the boil."

I took the flowers back into the sitting room and, as directed, put them down carefully ("On that little mat please, Sheila.") on the table by the window.

Mrs. Dudley is the only person I know now who actually has people to tea in the old-fashioned, formal way. I looked with pleasure at the small table laid with a white, lace-edged cloth, the delicate china and the knives and spoons with their mother-of-pearl handles. There were two sorts of tiny sandwiches (cucumber, and egg and cress), scones with clotted cream and jam, and two sorts of cake (an iced sponge and a rich fruit cake). Elsie had surpassed herself. She came in with the large silver teapot and the smaller hot-water jug on a tray. The tea ceremony is, in its way, as traditional as any Japanese one: a little hot water poured into the cup, rinsed round to warm it and poured into the slop basin; the heavy teapot (which I knew from past experience always dribbled just a little) that had to be held at a certain angle away from the cloth so that it wouldn't drip on it; the milk in last, of course, and the sugar always to be offered and always refused.

Mrs. Dudley watched the proceedings with an attentive eye and gave a tiny nod of approval when I'd accomplished it satisfactorily. She then put me through the customary, brisk inquiry about

Michael, Thea and Alice, which I knew was merely skirmishing before she got down to the real business of the meeting, as it were.

"So what's all this about Josephine Hamilton, then?"

"I expect you heard that the inquest said it was accidental death."

"And what do you think?"

"Well—I think it probably was."

"Probably? That's not what I heard."

"Well," I said again, "there was some problem about the wire being cut, but that was all explained at the inquest, and the coroner was quite satisfied."

Mrs. Dudley gave a short laugh. "Marcus Barrington! He's about as much use as a chocolate fireguard!"

I looked at her in amazement at this colloquial turn of phrase.

"I believe that's what dear Delia calls it—it struck me as a very colorful and accurate metaphor. I certainly wouldn't trust *his* judgment on any legal matter. How he came to be appointed coroner is, and always will be, a mystery to me."

"Still," I said, getting involved in a discussion I didn't really want, as always happens with Mrs. Dudley, "I do think it *was* most likely an accident. I mean, who would want to kill poor Jo? Everyone loved her."

"Not everyone." She paused to spread a scone with cream and jam. "Not everyone by any means."

"Who? Who could possibly dislike Jo?"

"Esther Nicholson for one."

"Esther? But she's Jo's sister!"

"What has that got to do with it?" Mrs. Dudley said sharply.

"But why?"

"She has always been bitterly jealous of her—the beautiful, talented older sister. Even as a young girl Esther was plain and very dull. You must remember that."

"Well, yes," I said, remembering guiltily several occasions in our youth when Esther had been excluded from some activity or other because someone said she was "dim" or "boring." "I suppose she must have felt left out sometimes."

"Exactly. And, of course, her parents made it very plain that Josephine was their favorite. I remember Margaret Howard saying frequently what a disappointment Esther was after her brilliant older sister."

"Poor Esther," I said. "I'm afraid we weren't very nice to her."

"And then there was the business with Gordon Nicholson."

"Gordon?"

"Oh yes, he was madly in love with Josephine; begged her to marry him several times."

"I never knew that."

"Well, he was hardly likely to publish his disappointment. It would have been a good match. He was a professional man and his family was very well off. Have you heard of Nicholson's, the builders? Arnold Nicholson, Gordon's father, worked his way up from nothing—*his* father was a common laborer—so it wasn't a good family, but he made a great deal of money building those houses out beyond the marshes. He got the land for a song. He always had an eye for the main chance. Gordon takes after him in that way."

I thought of the talk about Gordon's deals with Dan Webster. "Yes," I said, "he's always had a head for business. But I can see why Jo rejected him—very much not her sort of person. It would have been impossible!"

"The Howards didn't see it in that way. They were very upset that Josephine had refused such a good offer, especially since she'd refused his cousin Clive before. They weren't at all well off. If you remember, Desmond Howard was only a bank clerk and they thought it would have been a marvelous match for their daughter."

"But still—I can't imagine it, Jo and Gordon!"

"They put a certain amount of pressure on her, and that is why she went off to London."

"I see. But then Esther went to work for Gordon."

"That was some years later. I believe she had always had some sort of romantic ideas about him, her sister's young man—I believe that often happens—and he was still unmarried."

"And you think he married her as second best?"

"I believe that often happens too."

"Poor Esther."

"Well, I suppose she had got what she wanted." Mrs. Dudley paused. "Sheila dear, will you very kindly cut me a piece of sponge—no, a little larger than that—and have some yourself. You've eaten almost nothing. I do hope you are not on one of those stupid diets."

I cut myself a piece of sponge and assured her that, indeed, I was making an excellent tea.

"Of course," Mrs. Dudley went on, "getting what we want is not always what we *thought* we wanted."

I considered this aphoristic statement for a moment and then said, "It couldn't work, of course. If Esther knew that Jo was the love of his life and he'd only married her as a sort of substitute, she'd always feel inferior. And I suppose it was bad enough when Jo was in London leading that glamorous life, but, in a way it must have been much worse when she came back to Taviscombe with Charlie—who was so charismatic—and was there under Esther's nose every day, so to speak."

Mrs. Dudley nodded. "Exactly. And it hasn't helped that Simon, her own son, obviously preferred the company of his aunt to that of his mother."

"Oh dear." I absently took another slice of sponge. "I can see why Esther might very well hate her sister, but I really can't see her *killing* her."

"You think she is too stupid to choose such a recherché method?"

"Well, yes—it does seem a little, well, *inventive* for Esther."

"Ah," Mrs. Dudley said triumphantly, "but I happen to know that she had just had some electrical work done and that the electrician had warned her about the dangers of having wiring in a place where it might become damaged."

"Steve Webber?"

"He did happen to mention it when he came to put in a new switch for me."

"He doesn't think Jo's death was an accident," I said, resisting the temptation to lick the icing from my fingers, and wiping them decorously on my table napkin. "He thinks the wire was cut deliberately."

"Precisely," Mrs. Dudley said, "and he is a very experienced electrician."

"But at the inquest they said it was probably that heavy, metal cash box that cut the wire."

"Oh, the inquest!" Mrs. Dudley waved it aside. "I have no opinion of that ridiculous procedure. I've no doubt it suited them to call it an accident— less bother all round, typical of the slipshod way things are done today."

I ignored this slight on the criminal justice system. "But Esther!" I protested. "No, I really can't believe that."

"She adored that tiresome husband of hers and you must have noticed how oddly she has been behaving since he died."

"Well, yes, in a way, but that's only natural. It must have been a dreadful shock to have him collapsing like that."

"The man had had a serious heart condition for years. It can hardly have been unexpected, even to someone as stupid as Esther Nicholson."

"But she hardly ever went to the stables; she may not have gone that day."

"Has anyone asked her?"

"I suppose Inspector Morris may have done."

"*Inspector* Morris," Mrs. Dudley said scornfully. "What use is he? Why is Roger not looking into things?"

"He's based in Taunton now," I said apologetically, "though he is still taking an interest in it."

"That is all very well, but with a murderer on the loose, are we in Taviscombe to be considered less worthy of protection than the people of *Taunton*?"

There seemed to be no answer to that and, with Mrs. Dudley now in full Lady Bracknell mode, I was glad that Elsie came in just then to remove the tea things so that I could decently take my leave.

"Dear Sheila," Mrs. Dudley said as I bent to kiss her, "remember, all this dieting is bad for the health, especially at your age."

"Your mother really does know how to put the knife in," I said to Rosemary when I reported back to her. "That remark about dieting was pure malice!"

"You really should be used to it after nearly sixty years," Rosemary said, laughing.

"I know," I said ruefully, "but she gets to me every time. And what's all this about picking up phrases from Delia? I couldn't believe my ears!"

"Oh, that's Delia's latest ploy, spending time with Great-Grandma. It drives Jilly and Roger mad, which, of course, it's meant to. 'She's always beautifully behaved with *me*,' Mother says whenever any of us complain about how impossible Delia is. And 'She reminds me very much of what I was like at her age.' I mean, come on!"

"Oh dear, the deviousness of little girls," I said.

"She stuffs herself with cakes and things when she's there, just when Jill's trying so hard to get the children to eat healthily. Mother simply encourages her, of course, and Delia always comes away with extra pocket money—for doing well at school, that sort of thing!"

"Well, I suppose it's a new interest for your mother."

"Oh, by the way," Rosemary said, "Simon's been able to fix the date for Jo's funeral. It's going to be on the twenty-ninth at two thirty. St. James's, of course, and then at the County, like Charlie's do. Poor boy, that's the third funeral he's had to arrange. Jo wasn't up to doing Charlie's, so Simon did that, as well as his father's. I think it's all getting to him. He really did look awful when I saw him yesterday."

"Poor Simon," I said. "Everyone does rely on him. I'll go with Thea, of course, and I expect Michael will be able to get away."

But, as it happened I wasn't able to go to Jo's funeral. The day before, I came down with the particularly horrible feverish cold that had been going round Taviscombe—the sort of cold when all you can do is crawl miserably into bed and stay there. I did manage to phone Rosemary to tell her.

"Is there anything I can do?" she asked. "I could easily pop round this morning."

"No, it's fine," I croaked. "Thea, bless her, has been in and seen to the animals, and she's making me hot drinks and soup and things. Do please tell Simon how sorry I am not to be there, but I really can't make it. My throat's raw and I'm at the streaming stage. I've gone through one box of tissues already. Thea's made me some lemon and honey and I'm living on aspirin and Vick. . ." I broke off with a fit of coughing, and Rosemary, murmuring comforting words, rang off.

Putting down the phone, I sipped some of the lemon and honey, took some more aspirin and moved a reluctant Foss from under the duvet so that I could pull it up over my head and try to get some sleep.

I felt marginally better the next day and able to listen quite sensibly to Rosemary's account of the funeral.

"It was exactly the same as Charlie's, same hymns and everything. Simon told me that's what she wanted. Some of the same horsey people were there and some theater people—I recognized a few of them—and one of them said a few words. The church was more or less full and most people went on afterwards."

"I'm so glad," I said. "I just wish I could have been there too."

"I tell you who wasn't," Rosemary said.

"Who?"

"Esther."

"Really!"

"Apparently she wasn't well enough—she has the same bug as you. So really it was just Simon, Liz and Peggy. Oh, and Vicky. I think she was a bit put out at the girls from the stables being counted as 'family,' but they certainly had more right than she has."

"Especially Liz. She was almost like a daughter to Jo and Charlie."

"I think that's always riled Vicky. Apparently she was *very* put out that Liz had been left the house as well as a share of the stables."

"She really is so like Gordon—money, money, money!"

"And she was networking—if that's what they call it—after the funeral, chatting up some of the theater people. I think she wanted them for this program of hers, the one Jo wouldn't do. Oh yes, and she was asking after you, something she wants *you* for."

"Well, at least I've avoided that," I said. "But I would have liked to be there, just to say good-bye to Jo."

"Anyway, how are you?" Rosemary asked.

"I think the worst's over," I said cautiously. "It was pretty violent but mercifully short. My head feels full of cotton wool and my sinuses are all bunged up, but my temperature's down, so I can function enough to get up and see to the animals. And Thea's been marvelous. She's brought me some gorgeous fish pie for my supper, just what I feel like."

"Well, don't go overdoing things. You must take care"—she paused—"especially at *your* age, as Mother would doubtless say."

But I should have realized that I wasn't going to escape Vicky that easily. I'd just put the fish pie in the microwave to warm it up when she rang.

"Oh, Sheila, I was sorry to miss you at the funeral," she said, "because we need to finalize your contribution to my Victorian writers program."

In my weakened state I hardly felt equal to protesting that I hadn't agreed to any contribution. She went on to outline the "scope," as she called it, of the program and what she needed me to say ". . . in relation to the other contributors. I've been so lucky to get Christine Marshall—she wrote that excellent book on the Brontës; it was *very* well reviewed—and Freda Anderson on George Eliot. So if you concentrate on Mrs. Gaskell, along the lines I've indicated, and just *touch* on Charlotte Yonge . . . I won't want much on her—all that religion puts people off. So if you could, let me have a script, about four thousand words, though we can cut it if necessary, by the beginning of next week. I'll book a parking space for you. That's splendid."

She'd rung off before I could make any effective protest, so I just gave up and switched on the microwave, feeling somehow that she'd quite spoiled my pleasure in the fish pie.

Chapter Fifteen

When, a week later, I got to the BBC studios in Bristol, I found Vicky very much in charge.

"I had to come down for a special meeting this morning," she said importantly, "so it was convenient to stay on to do your piece. I've booked a studio."

I have to admit that Vicky's very good at her job. She did the recording briskly and efficiently, with only a few interruptions, mostly technical and about sound levels and so forth.

"Right," she said when we'd finished, "I've got a spare half hour, so shall we go and get a cup of tea and a bun in the canteen? That's unless you'd rather have a polystirene cup of not-very-nice coffee from the machine."

I opted gratefully for the tea and a rather nice slice of Dundee cake. For a while Vicky talked about the program and about other programs she had done or was proposing to do, and I listened in a sort of daze. I listened more attentively when she began talking about Jo.

"It's absolutely ridiculous that she should have left the house to that girl. A valuable property like that should have gone to one of the family. I didn't expect her to leave me anything—we never got on; Simon was always her favorite—but to leave it to a stable girl!"

"I think Liz was rather more than a stable girl," I said placatingly. "Really, she's devoted her life to the place."

"Well, she's got a share of the business. I'd have thought that was more than enough."

"Simon seems quite happy about the arrangement."

"Oh, Simon—he's hopeless about any sort of business."

"He is an accountant," I said. "That's business, after all."

Vicky gave a short laugh. "Not a very good one, from what I've heard. Mother says he's always having trouble trying to keep up with things at work. Mind you, he never wanted to go into accountancy. Father made him."

"What did he want to do?" I asked.

"Oh, he had some silly idea of helping Jo and Charlie. You can imagine what Father thought about that!"

I could imagine it very well. "Perhaps he'd have been happier doing that."

"Happier!" Vicky said scornfully. "What's that got to do with it? No, my little brother's always been a bit odd. There was that girlfriend—what was her name?—Julie something. We quite thought they'd get engaged. It would have been a good match; her father was one of the partners. But that came to nothing."

"I thought she went away to London," I said.

"Yes, she did, but that was after she'd broken it off with Simon. We never knew why. And I'd like to know what he does in London when he comes up to stay with me. Oh, I know he goes to a few theaters, but some evenings he doesn't, and he's out nearly every afternoon. When I ask him where he's been, he just says walking round London."

"Well, perhaps he is. I must say I like just wandering around looking at things when I'm up there."

"Oh, that's different—you write books," Vicky said, as if that covered any sort of eccentricity.

"Well, he's certainly putting a lot of time in at the stables," I said.

"I suppose he might marry that girl," Vicky said thoughtfully. "At least it would keep that house in the family."

Driving back up Whiteladies Road I decided I didn't want to face the motorway, so I went up onto the Downs to take the old-fashioned A38 home. As I scrabbled in my purse for the money for the toll on the suspension bridge, I considered what Vicky had said about Simon. I could see why she couldn't understand Simon's wish to "walk about London," something she would never have thought of doing. Simon, I now realized, has always been something of a dreamer; pushed by his father into a career he disliked and wasn't good at, he must have often felt the need to escape from the realities of life. I suppose that's why he spent so much time at the stables. I wondered what the future held for him now that his father had died.

Going out of Bristol I suddenly remembered seeing Jo at Temple Mead station and how drawn and anxious she had looked when she thought she was unobserved. I wondered what the "tiresome business" was that she had to face that day. I'd learned so much about her life since she died that I began to feel as if I'd never really known her. But then, how could we possibly say that we knew anybody? It was all too confusing, so I found some soothing music on the radio and concentrated on my driving.

When I got back home the animals rushed out madly into the garden as if they'd been shut up in the house for days rather than hours. I saw with some irritation that it was now raining, so I'd have muddy paw marks all over the kitchen. It had been a long day; I suddenly felt very tired, too tired even to make a cup of tea or pour a drink, and simply sat at the kitchen table, not moving. It occurred to me that I'd been getting old without really noticing it and after doing something unusual, out of my old routine, I no longer had the resilience to pick myself up straightaway. A sharp bark (Tris wanting to come in) got me to my feet and, reaching for his towel, I went to let him in.

"So how did you get on?"

Rosemary and I have the habit, and have had for years, of phoning each other most mornings. Thea or Michael, bless them, ring every day to see if I'm "all right," but it's not quite the same. Just chat I suppose, but it's an exchange of news, thoughts and a good moan, something you can only really share with someone of your own generation, especially someone you've grown up with.

"Oh, it went quite well," I said. "Whatever reservations I might have about Vicky—and I can't say I care for her as a person—she's very good at her job, very professional. But *so* different from Simon!"

"Oh, she's always taken after Gordon, though I can't say Simon takes after Esther, thank goodness!"

"No, he's always seemed the odd one out in that family. I mean, he's always been wonderfully patient with Esther and has tried hard to be a good son, but somehow . . ."

"I know what you mean," Rosemary said. "You sort of feel he's never fitted in."

"Vicky was telling me about how he used to spend days, when he was staying with her, just wandering around London. That is the sort of thing *we* would enjoy, but can you imagine Gordon or Esther doing it! Or Vicky, of course. She was very scornful."

"She would be."

"She did say that Simon was pushed into his accountancy job by Gordon. Simon never wanted to do it."

"Oh, he hates it. Jack used to tell me how terribly difficult Simon found it all when he was just starting with his firm. He took ages to pick things up and was very slow. Jack, bless him, felt sorry for the boy and did his best to help. By the time Simon left to go to Frobisher and King—I think Gordon exerted a bit of influence to get him in there—he was more or less competent. But it's obvious he's pretty miserable and should never have been forced into it."

"Perhaps now Gordon's dead, Simon can do something else. I don't suppose Esther would mind, and, anyway, he's in his thirties for goodness' sake; he doesn't have to consult her!"

"But what would he do? Accountancy's all he's trained for."

"He could take over the stables," I suggested. "He spends all his spare time there and now he owns the biggest share of them—well, why not?"

"It's a thought. Jo would have liked that. I wonder if that's what she had in mind."

"I don't see why he couldn't make a go of it," I said. "He's been riding all his life, though I don't know about teaching people, and he's been doing the books already, so he'd go on seeing to that side of things."

We discussed this possibility enthusiastically for some time, planning a splendid new life for Simon, until Rosemary said, "It would be perfect, but I wonder if Gordon hasn't sapped his confidence too much for him to change direction now."

"You know him best. You could sound him out—see if he's been thinking about it."

"I might just do that," Rosemary said.

I'd only just put the phone down when Thea rang.

"Sheila, could you do me a favor? Could you take Alice and me up to the stables on Saturday afternoon? My car's got to go in to have the transmission seen to and I can't have the Land Rover because Michael's got a clay shoot."

"Of course, I'd love to. How nice that you and Alice are riding together now."

"Well, it's her first proper one-hour ride, off the leading rein, so I thought I'd go along. Anyway, I do enjoy it, especially now I don't get so stiff every time."

I was quite glad to have a reason for going to the stables to see how things were going there.

"It's only an hour," I said to Thea as we arrived, "so it's not worth going away and coming back. I've got a book."

"Come *along* Mummy!" Alice said, tugging at Thea's arm. "Gran, come and see Cracker. He really knows me now."

I followed them into the stable yard. "You carry on, Thea," I said, as Peggy led the horses out. "I'll go and pay for the ride—my treat."

I watched them out of sight and then went into the office. Simon was sitting at the desk. I noticed that the tangle of wires had now been boxed in and there was a new set of switches. I wondered how Simon felt, sitting there. But I suppose life does go on and they needed the office.

"Hello," I said. "I've come to pay for Thea and Alice's ride."

Simon looked up from some papers he'd been studying and smiled. "Hello, Sheila. How are you? Rosemary said you hadn't been well."

"Oh, I'm fine now. It was that horrible bug that was going around. I was so sorry not to be able to get to the funeral. Jo was a good friend and I would have liked to say good-bye."

"It was very well attended. People came from all over."

"I'm so glad."

There was an awkward silence; then I said, "How are things going here? Liz and Peggy seem to have everything well in hand."

"Yes." He took up the subject gratefully. "They've been marvelous—Liz especially. I think we can make a go of it. We've got plans for riding holidays for the young. I thought we could use those outbuildings at the back and make a sort of dormitory. Peggy assures me all young girls want to sleep in dormitories! Other stables do it. It's a good source of income in itself and can bring new people in on a permanent basis." He spoke enthusiastically. "Or, at least," he went on, reverting to his own more hesitant manner, "that's what they tell me."

"I think it's a splendid idea," I said, "and I can think of several little girls of my acquaintance who'll be nagging their parents as soon as you've got it up and running."

He smiled. "I'll get you to spread the word as soon as we have it sorted out."

"Anyway," I said, "I must let you get on." I put the money for the ride down on the desk and went away.

I got back into the car and began to read my book in a desultory way, but I couldn't concentrate, so I put it away and looked around me. Simon had come out of the office and was standing with Liz, deep in conversation as they looked down across the fields. She was talking very earnestly about something, and he was smiling and nodding. At one point he put his arm round her shoulder in a friendly gesture, and the look she gave him made it suddenly very obvious to me how she felt about him. I wondered whether Simon even noticed it; probably not. He patted her shoulder absently, smiled again and went back into the office. Liz stood for several minutes, quite still, leaning on the rail; then she too went inside, into the stable yard.

I was still considering what I'd seen, when I was aware of another vehicle approaching. In my rear mirror I saw that it was Dan Webster's Mitsubishi. Some instinct made me crouch lower in my seat and appear to be buried in my book, though I needn't have bothered since he took no notice and went briskly past me into the office.

On an impulse I got out of the car, shutting the door as quietly as I could, and went up towards the stables. Cautiously, I edged as near as I could get to the door in the hope of hearing something, but, although I could catch the murmur of voices, I couldn't make out any of the conversation. I stood there for a moment and then, feeling rather ridiculous, I moved away. When Liz came out I was standing by the gate leading to the bridle path.

"Hello," she greeted me. "Are you waiting for Alice?"

"Alice and Thea," I said, thankful that she hadn't seen me doing my amateur spy act. "They're both out today. It's a beautiful day for it."

"Mm." She raised her face to the sun and smiled happily. "It's a perfect day."

We chatted for a while about nothing in particular, both of us content just to bask in the sunshine, gazing over the peaceful countryside. Our mood was broken by the appearance of Dan Webster coming out of the office. He was obviously not in a good mood and, as he left, he called back over his shoulder, "Well, just you think about it. We both have a great deal more to discuss. I'll be back."

He got into his car, slamming the door with some violence, and drove away.

"What a disagreeable man," I said.

Liz nodded but didn't say anything.

"I'm sure Jo was keen to get Tarquin away from him," I suggested.

"He's a beautiful horse," Liz said, "and he's come on wonderfully. He just needed proper handling."

"Well, he's certainly better away from that man," I said. "Does he still ride from here?"

"No, I don't think he rides at all now. Jo said he

only did it to get in with the hunting set—something to do with business, I think."

I wanted very much to ask what sort of business he had with Simon, but I couldn't think of any way of introducing such a question casually into the conversation. The appearance of the riders brought an end to it anyway, and I was left to speculate.

Alice was very full of her ride and Thea almost as enthusiastic.

"It's ridiculous not to take advantage of the nice weather while it lasts. Soon it'll be winter and horribly cold and wet," she said. "I think I'll just go and make another booking for us both."

When she came out again she was looking very puzzled.

"I don't know what's the matter with Simon," she said. "He seemed miles away—hardly took in what I was saying. I had to ask him for a booking a couple of times until it got through to him."

"How extraordinary," I said. "He was quite all right when I saw him before."

"He looked as if something had upset him quite badly. He pulled himself together and apologized, but it was all a bit odd. Anyway, shall we go back and have some tea? You'll stay, won't you, Sheila?"

Alice hung on my arm. "Do come to tea, Gran, and then I can tell you all about Cracker. He trotted really *fast*. . . ."

When I got home I mulled over what I'd heard about Dan Webster and what he could have been talking to Simon about. What, indeed, had he been saying to leave Simon so upset? Jim Robinson had said that Webster was into property, presumably in a big way, but I couldn't imagine how that might affect Simon. True, he'd inherited the stables and the land all round, but I didn't think small riding stables would tempt someone like Dan Webster, and no one could ever get planning permission to build in the fields, so it couldn't be that. I remembered seeing his Mitsubishi up on the moors beside Jo's Land Rover. Obviously whatever it was that Webster wanted he'd been pursuing for a long time, since I didn't think, somehow, that particular meeting had just been about Tarquin. It all seemed very strange.

My thoughts were rudely interrupted by a noise from the kitchen. Foss, in an attempt to get at an impertinent blue tit that had been pecking at the putty in the window, had leapt onto the windowsill, knocking down a handsome coleus plant I'd been nurturing, and smashing the pot. Undeterred by this, he was still on the windowsill, chittering angrily at the birds on the feeder.

As I resignedly swept up the soil and pottery fragments, I suddenly thought of Liz and the smile she had given Simon. It occurred to me that Vicky's suggestion, though given for the wrong reason, might very well be a happy ending for both of them.

Chapter Sixteen

"I was going to circulate the lottery information," Anthea said, backing me up into a corner in the post office, "but Muriel, who said she'd do the photocopying, had to go up to Reading because her sister's had a fall and there's no one else to look after their father. George *says* he'll get it done for us—he's got a photocopier at home, so it won't cost us anything—but he's not very reliable. Anyway, Derek is going to see to the application itself. He used to be something very high up in insurance, so I suppose he should be competent to do that. It's been most annoying—all these delays when I really wanted us to get moving *quickly*. There will be so many applications and we mustn't miss our chance, but push ahead."

Anthea obviously saw the whole lottery system as a kind of race where the prizes would go to the fastest, who would gain their advantage by elbowing the other competitors out of the way.

"I'm sure Derek will do it admirably," I said, seizing the least controversial thread of her narrative.

"But what we *must* do," she continued, "is to

start to raise our share of the money as soon as possible. I'm calling a committee meeting for next week—Tuesday, I thought—and I do hope people will come with a lot of good ideas."

"I don't think I can manage Tuesday," I said.

Anthea gave an exclamation of impatience. "It's always the same," she said crossly. "It's practically impossible to arrange any sort of meeting at a time to suit everyone. Don't tell me you're off on holiday again!"

"No, nothing like that. It's just that I've got several appointments fixed for that day and I really can't cancel them."

"Oh, is that all," Anthea said, brushing my excuse to one side. "We can have the meeting in the evening, then. I'm sure you'll be able manage that! Say seven o'clock?"

"Oh, not seven," I said. "Don't you remember, all the people who eat in the evening do find that difficult—you either have to eat too early or too late."

"Oh really, such nonsense! I have my main meal at midday—so much better for you. Well, in that case we'll make it six; it won't go on that long."

"No," I said doubtfully, remembering several acrimonious meetings that had gone on until very late in the evening. "No, that should be fine."

"I'll give George a reminder so that you can all have the lottery information before the meeting. And remember," Anthea said briskly, "lots of new, bright ideas!"

"Actually," I said, "do we know how much

money we need to raise? I mean, what's the whole thing going to cost? How much are we applying for?"

"That's another thing," Anthea said with some annoyance. "Steve Webber was going to come and give me an estimate, but when I rang, his wife said he'd gone off to Barnstaple to do some big electrical job there and wouldn't be back for a fortnight."

"In that case," I suggested, "wouldn't it be better to wait until we've got the estimate before we have the meeting? I mean, Derek can't make an application until we know how much we actually want."

"Not at all," Anthea said firmly. "We need to have plans made so that we can start raising our part of the money as soon as possible."

Fortunately the post office queue, which had been building up while this conversation was going on, now impinged on our space and gave me an excuse for bringing our talk to a conclusion.

"So," I said to Michael when he came round to saw up an old apple tree that had fallen down in the garden, "poor Derek's been lumbered with this lottery thing. I should think he must regret being retired, what with all the jobs around the house that Edna has been saving up for him over the years, and now Anthea nagging him!"

"And his work on the parish council," Michael said. "I suppose it's the usual case of the willing horse."

"I don't think anyone forced to do something by Anthea could be called willing," I said.

"Oh yes, I meant to tell you," Michael went on. "He told me that the council—I mean the planning committee of the District Council—have decided to change the District Plan to redesignate some of the land near the stables from agricultural to potential-development use. This means that it *could* be built on."

"Really? I haven't seen anything about it in the *Free Press*."

"No, they have to let the parish councils know first—and some other people too; I can't remember who—before the public get to know about it."

"So, technically, someone could build houses on the fields round the stables. That's awful!"

"Well, Jo and Charlie, and now Simon, own all the fields immediately next to the stables. Simon would never sell, so it should be all right."

"I suppose so. But, all the same, it's horrid to think of houses, or worse, in those beautiful fields."

"It's not a conservation area," Michael said, "and people have to live somewhere."

"Yes, I know that, but there's a lot of places on the outskirts of Taviscombe where they've been building already, so a few more houses over there wouldn't make any difference. And this is agricultural land—pasture anyway."

"Well, as I said, Simon won't sell and those fields go right up to the edge of the woods, so that particular spot is safe."

"Thank goodness."

"I expect the council will grant planning permission if the developer, whoever it is, promises to build a certain amount of affordable housing. It's the sort of deal they make."

"Of course!" I said. "That's what that horrible man Dan Webster must have wanted!"

"Dan Webster?"

"Yes, I've seen him up at the stables several times, to see Simon, and Jo too. I'm sure he was pestering them to sell those fields. He sounded really unpleasant when he was up there talking to Simon a few days ago."

"Unpleasant?"

"Yes, as he was going I heard him say there was a great deal still to discuss, and he said he'd be back. It sounded quite threatening, and Thea said Simon seemed really upset when she saw him afterwards."

"It's certainly the sort of deal Webster might want to make. It's the kind of thing he does. They say he usually gets what he wants somehow or other. But I don't think we need worry about Simon. I'm sure he'd never give in to someone like Webster. Anyway, I must get on. I think I'll have to use the band saw on this lot. It's not very sharp, but it's better than the big one."

As I went into the house to make Michael a cup of tea, I thought about Simon and wondered about his ability to stand up to Dan Webster. I was sure he wouldn't want to sell the fields, but I wondered just how well he might stand up to that sort of bullying. Jo would have done. Presumably that was what Webster wanted when they met up on the moor; it would hardly have been about Tarquin. No, Jo would have seen him off. But if Simon had been as upset as Thea said he was when he'd had just a short meeting with Webster, how would he cope with "I'll be back," which was obviously going to be a continuing attack. I wondered if there was anyone who could bolster up Simon's self-confidence and stiffen his resistance. I thought I might have a word with Rosemary, who knows him better than most.

Tuesday's meeting at Brunswick Lodge went off more or less as I'd expected. Although George had managed to photocopy the lottery information, there was a certain amount of grumbling about not knowing how much the job would cost.

"We need the actual *figures*," Derek kept saying. "It's not good asking me to do anything without them, because I can't."

"How can we know what to raise," Maureen said plaintively, "if we don't know the *proportion* required?"

The phrase obviously pleased her since she repeated it several times, as Derek kept reiterating his need for the figures. Anthea, not one to encourage democratic comment, simply ignored them and, raising her voice slightly, brought the meeting to order.

"What we have to do," she said firmly, "is to consider all possible ways of raising our share of the money—whatever," she said, glancing sternly at Maureen, "that may be. Now, I do hope all of you have come armed with some original ideas."

As usual, after such a request, there was dead silence all round the table.

"Well, come along," Anthea said impatiently. "Surely *somebody's* done some thinking and come up with something."

Gradually the usual suggestions emerged: raffles, auctions, bring and buy sales, sponsored walks, a concert. All such ideas were tentatively proposed by one member and promptly disparaged by the rest.

"This is getting us nowhere," Anthea said. "Sheila, you haven't said anything yet. Surely you've got some suggestion to make!"

"Well," I said, "why don't we simply ask for donations? People will usually give you something if you ask them directly, and I'm sure we'd make just as much money that way."

There was a brief moment's shocked silence at this revolutionary idea, and then Anthea said scathingly, "Well, really, if you're just going to make silly suggestions like that . . ."

"Why don't we have a break for a cup of tea?" Maureen suggested. "I'll just go and put the kettle on."

She went off into the kitchen, closely followed by Derek's wife, Edna, a reluctant member of the committee who only ever came to the meetings to make sure Derek wasn't going to be put upon (her words) by Anthea. While we were having our tea, people broke up into little groups and I went over to talk to Derek.

"Derek," I said, "have you ever come across a man called Dan Webster?"

His expression changed from its usual bland amiability to a positive scowl.

"Yes, I have," he said, "and I hope he's not a friend of yours because a nastier piece of work I've yet to meet."

"No," I said hastily, "certainly not. In fact I think he's trying to put pressure on a friend and I'm rather worried."

"Putting pressure on people is something he does all the time," Derek said. "That place of his up at Upper Barton, now that's a case in point."

"Really?"

"Yes. It belonged to elderly friends of mine, and when Edgar died last year we all wondered what Margaret—that's his wife—would do. It was much too big for her and really, to be honest, needed a lot done to it. But this Webster man heard about it and badgered her to sell it to him. Now, there was no need for her to make a big decision like that straightaway—at a time like that when she was still grieving. But he kept on at her; said she wouldn't get a good price for it because of all the work it needed; hassled her until she gave in. Unfortunately, we were away just then, visiting our son in Canada, and when her nephew up in Doncaster—they didn't have any children—got to hear about it, it was too late. Webster paid a fair price, but it was the way he went about it that made us so mad."

"They say he always gets what he wants," I said, "somehow or other."

"Like I said, nasty piece of work. There was another thing too."

"Really?"

"I didn't deal with it myself, but a colleague of mine said that he bought a big old house just outside Taunton. It was very run-down and would have taken a fortune to put right. Anyway, Webster applied for permission to pull it down, but it was a grade two–listed building, so he didn't get it. Then it started to get vandalized—I wouldn't have put it past him to have organized that—and then there was a fire. The whole house wasn't burnt down, but there was a lot of damage. That's when my colleague was involved over the insurance. Finally it got into such a state that it was downright dangerous and *had* to be pulled down, which, of course, is what he'd wanted in the first place."

"You think he arranged the whole thing?" I asked.

"Well, let's say I think he helped things along. Nothing could be proved, of course. People like Webster are good at covering their tracks."

"I can imagine. So what happened?"

"There was quite a bit of land with the house, so he had some plans drawn up with a couple of starter homes as a sop to the council and built half a dozen fair-sized houses on the site."

"And made a great deal of money?"

"Exactly. So tell your friend to be careful."

Anthea, who'd been getting restless at the prolonged tea-drinking, made efforts to chivy us all back to the meeting, but George looked at his watch and said he had to be going, and several other people said they had to go too. Anthea was engaged in some sort of argument with Maureen ("For goodness' sake, the proportion doesn't *matter*!"), so I took the opportunity to slip away while her back was turned.

I hadn't had an opportunity to talk to Rosemary about Simon, but when I ran into her at the garden center, it seemed like a good moment.

"I've found these gorgeous hellebores," she said. "Wonderful, *sinister* colors they'll have, and, although I usually have a malign effect on practically everything I plant, I really couldn't resist. How about you? Have you found anything?"

"Not really. I just wanted some more heathers to fill in the gaps on that bank by the gate. It's always nice to have something blooming in the winter. Actually, have you got time for a coffee? There's something I want to talk to you about."

"There's nothing special I should be doing and they do rather nice Danish pastries in the café here."

When we were sitting down Rosemary said, "So, what is it?"

"Have you seen anything of Simon lately?" I asked.

"I saw him last weekend when I went to collect

Delia from the stables—she practically *lives* there now—and he was there then."

"He does spend a lot of time up there now."

"Well, he is a part owner and they do need his help—not just at weekends either."

"You haven't found out," I asked, "if he's had any thoughts about working at the stables full-time?"

"Well, I did sort of broach the subject when I saw him, but he just said he didn't think they could afford for him to take a salary out of the business, so he felt he had to soldier on with the accountancy."

"Such a pity," I said.

"Well, I suppose the money from his proper job does help, though he and Liz do seem to have some really good ideas about expanding the business. They seem to be getting on really well. I sometimes wonder. . . ."

"Oh, she's obviously deeply devoted to him," I said, and I told her what Vicky had said.

"It's the right idea," Rosemary agreed, "if for the wrong reason—*typical* Vicky—and it would be perfect for both of them. Just what Simon needs, a nice girl looking up to him and thinking he's marvelous."

I smiled. "She certainly does that all right. But there's something else I'm really worried about." I explained what Michael had said about the change of use of the land around the stables and what Derek had told me about Dan Webster. "If he wants to develop that land—and I'm sure he's got his eye on it—he'll keep on at Simon. He's such a *strong* character and could be really threatening. I don't know if Simon can stand up to him."

"Simon cared so much for Jo and Charlie," Rosemary said, "he couldn't betray them like that."

"Well, Thea said Simon was very upset when she saw him just after Dan Webster had been there, and Derek said Webster was the sort of man who always got what he wanted. I'm afraid he's just going to *hound* poor Simon until he gives in."

"Not," Rosemary said firmly, "if we all stand by him and buoy him up. I'll have a word with Jack. I know Simon respects his advice."

"And I'll get Michael to see if there's anything in the will that might stop him selling," I said.

"Cheer up," Rosemary said. "I'm sure that all of us together will be a match for Dan Webster! Meanwhile," she went on, "I'll keep an eye on Liz and Simon and see if I can promote *that* little affair. A Christmas wedding would be nice."

"There are times, Rosemary Dudley," I said, "when you remind me irresistibly of your mother."

Chapter Seventeen

I'd been having Sunday lunch with Michael and Thea and, while Thea and Alice were outside seeing to the chickens, I took the opportunity to have a word with Michael. I told him how worried I was about Dan Webster and asked him if there was anything in Jo's will that might prevent Simon's selling the land.

"No, it was left to him absolutely," Michael said. "It would have been unusual for her to have done anything else."

"It's just that I think the Webster man had been trying to get Jo to sell and she might have wanted to make sure that Simon couldn't."

"But the change of use has only just been granted," Michael said, "so there'd have been no point in his trying to buy the land then, before Jo died."

"But, just suppose," I said, "that Webster had got wind of the council's decision, before it was made public; he'd have been one step ahead of anyone else."

"Well, yes, but . . ."

"And Dan Webster was hand in glove with

Gordon, who was on the planning committee, so it's not impossible that he *did* know what was going to happen."

"I'm sure that's slanderous," Michael said. "Promise me you won't go around saying things like that!"

"No, really. If you think about it, Webster might have been acting with Gordon—a sort of front man because Gordon couldn't be seen to be profiting from a council decision. And then Gordon died, so Webster was able to have the whole scheme to himself. That's probably when he started to try to put the pressure on Jo. But *she* wasn't having it."

"So?"

"So, it was probably obvious that Jo would leave the stables and land to Simon, who Webster would think was an easy target."

"So?"

"*So*, perhaps Webster killed her."

"Oh, for goodness' sake, Ma," Michael said, "I thought you'd given up the idea of it being murder, after the inquest and after everything the coroner said."

"Mrs. Dudley doesn't think Marcus Barrington is competent," I said provocatively. "She said she wouldn't trust his judgment on any legal matter."

"Oh really . . ."

"She said he was no more use than a chocolate fireguard."

"What!"

"I know. Apparently she's taken to picking up the latest colloquialisms from Delia."

"Good heavens."

"But seriously, it isn't *that* far-fetched. Webster's well-known for getting what he wants at any cost. It would have been quite easy. There's often no one in the office, especially when the rides are out, and he's been around the stables quite a lot with all the business about that horse."

"No, Ma," Michael said firmly, "I refuse to consider any of that and I strongly advise you to forget all about it."

I couldn't argue anymore because Alice came rushing in with a basket.

"Gran, do look. I've been collecting the eggs and there are some here for you!"

"Gently, Alice," Thea said, "or you'll break them. Only three today—they're starting to go off lay, but do have them. I'll go and find an egg box for them."

But as I took my eggs home I was still turning over in my mind the possibility that Dan Webster might have had something to do with Jo's death, though, for the moment at least, I didn't see any way of proving it.

I saw Roger a few days later at a concert at Brunswick Lodge. Anthea was mercifully having one of her feuds with Wendy Parker, who organizes them and was pointedly absent, so I didn't have to spend my time avoiding her and could concentrate on talking to Roger in the interval.

"I suppose the police aren't taking any more action about Jo's death," I said.

"Not after the inquest," Roger said. "That made it pretty clear it was an accident."

"And everybody's happy that it was?" I asked tentatively.

Roger looked at me sternly. "Now Sheila, don't try to make something out of nothing, just so you'll have something to worry away at!"

"No, no," I said hastily. "I suppose it's just having two accidents in the same place, one so soon after another."

"Just two tragic accidents," Roger said. "And in a place like a stable, especially with temperamental horses around, there's always a chance of something like that. As for poor Jo's death, well, that was obviously an accident waiting to happen."

"I suppose so. And Inspector Morris is quite satisfied?"

"Yes," Roger said firmly, "quite satisfied. Now, do you want another glass of this rather thin red wine or shall we get back to our seats? I'm looking forward to the Schumann. You don't very often have a chance to hear it."

Faced with such a determined effort to close the subject, I hardly felt it was possible to introduce my suspicions of Dan Webster. All through the rest of the concert I was turning over in my mind how I could find *something* that might back up my suspicions. But I realized, in the light of our conversation, that it would have to be something really conclusive to persuade Roger (and Bob Morris) to take me seriously.

*   *   *

The maddening thing about supermarkets is the way that, just when you think you know where everything is, they immediately move things around. Our local branch had recently had a refit (presumably for their convenience since it obviously wasn't for ours), and I was trying to discover where they'd put the olive oil, when someone behind me said wearily, "I don't suppose you've come across the cheese biscuits anywhere?"

I turned round and found that it was Eileen Butler, an old friend.

"Hello," I said. "How are you? It's been ages since I saw you."

"Oh, soldiering on. You know how it is. It's been a busy time of the year and I'm only just getting back to normal."

Eileen is married to a farmer, whose fields adjoin those belonging to the stables.

"Of course, you do farm holidays, don't you?"

"Well, you have to do something these days, farming being how it is."

"It must be hard work."

"It's not bad, but you have to be around all the time. I did want to get to poor Jo Hamilton's funeral—that was a dreadful thing—but we had some people coming in that day, so I couldn't get away."

"Yes, it was a terrible shock, especially so soon after Charlie's death."

"They were good neighbors and good friends. We'll miss them."

"I'm sure you'll get along with Jo's nephew,

Simon, who's taken over the stables. Do you know him?"

"We've seen him around for years, off and on, and had the occasional chat. He seems a pleasant young man. As a matter of fact, Will's been meaning to go over there and have a talk with him about something."

"Really?"

She hesitated for a moment, and then she said, "How well do you know him? It's a rather delicate matter and I know Will's worried about how he might react."

"Oh, Simon's a thoroughly nice person," I said. "I'm sure he'll be helpful if there's a problem."

"Will's had an offer for some of his fields. There's been some sort of new planning thing that means the land can be built on."

"Was the offer made by someone called Dan Webster?" I asked.

Eileen looked at me in surprise. "Yes, as a matter of fact it was. Do you know him?"

"Only by sight, but I've been hearing a lot about him lately." I hesitated. "So, how does Will feel about selling?"

"Oh no, he wouldn't hear of it. Said his mind was made up, even though this Webster man was very persistent and kept telephoning and coming round to the farm."

"Good for Will."

"Ours isn't a very big farm, as you know, and we couldn't afford to lose that many fields and still carry on. It's not so much Will—though it's always been his life and he does get a bit depressed at how things are going—but it's for the boys. Well, for Johnny; Craig's off to Bristol, working as a surveyor. But Johnny's never wanted to do anything else, ever since he was a toddler, following Will around the farm and riding in the cab of the tractor. He's wonderful with the animals. We still have a few beef cattle and some sheep; visitors like to see animals around the place when they're staying. No, Will would never agree to selling any of the land, even though this man offered a very fancy price."

"I can imagine."

"And, anyway, we wouldn't want a lot of houses or goodness knows what right next to us."

"No, I can see that."

"But we're wondering what Simon's going to do. I mean, Dan Webster's sure to have made him an offer and, well, if he accepts, then where will the houses be built? I mean, it'll be very awkward if they're right up against our fields."

"It would certainly affect your farm holidays," I said, "as well as everything else."

"That's right." She looked at me inquiringly. "So what do you think Simon's likely to do?"

"I'm sure he wouldn't want to sell," I said, "but, of course, I don't know the circumstances. He's only just taken over the stables, after all, so I suppose he's still finding his feet there."

Eileen nodded. "I can see that. Oh well, we'll just have to see what he says to Will."

"I do hope it all works out for you," I said. "I'd

hate to think of that man getting his hands on any of that land."

"What have you heard about him?"

"Just that he's a bully who likes to get his own way—a few things like that. I'm so glad Will is standing up to him."

I told Rosemary about my talk with Eileen.

"Well, good for them," she said. "Jack hasn't had a chance to speak to Simon yet, but I really can't believe he would ever sell those fields. I mean, from a practical point of view, apart from anything else, they need them for the horses. Grazing's expensive, and if they mean to expand . . ."

"Exactly. I'm sure it'll be all right. Besides," I added as a sudden thought struck me, "Simon must have inherited something from Gordon. There was a lot of money there and surely he won't have left everything to Esther."

"I think," Rosemary said, "he set up trusts for Vicky and for Simon, tying up the money somehow."

"Typical!" I said. "Making things difficult. For goodness' sake, they're not children, not even particularly young now. Just when Simon could use that money for the stables."

"I suppose," Rosemary said thoughtfully, "Gordon did it so that Simon couldn't give up accountancy."

"Imposing his wishes from beyond the grave! Can't Simon break the trust somehow?"

"I don't know. It probably hasn't occurred to him to try. You know how oppressed he was by his father."

"He might borrow from the bank against his expectations," I said. "I must ask Michael if that's possible."

"Talking of Simon and Gordon," Rosemary said, "have you seen Esther lately?"

"No, not for quite a while, which is odd, really, because I was forever running into her. How about you?"

"Well, yes I did. I saw her in the chemist—I wanted one of those heat patches for Jack's bad back, but, of course, he'll never use it—and I thought she looked very strained."

"Strained?"

"You know, sort of tense and anxious."

"Did you speak to her?"

"Very briefly; she didn't seem to want to talk."

"*That's* not like her!"

"Exactly. No, I asked her how she was, but, instead of going on like she usually does, she just said she was quite well and that was more or less that. It was even odder because I saw she'd been collecting some sort of medication, and you know how she loves telling you every last detail about any sort of illness she has."

"Very odd."

"I did ask her to come round for coffee one morning, but she said she was rather busy just now, and that's not like her either."

"I suppose she's still getting over Gordon's

death," I said. "It wasn't that long ago and it must have hit her very hard."

Strangely enough I ran into Esther the very next day. I'd gone down to the harbor, as I often do after I've finished the shopping, and I was sitting in the car, looking at a large container ship making its way slowly up the Bristol Channel, when I saw a figure leaning on the seawall. For a moment I didn't recognize her because it was the last place I'd have expected to see Esther, but there was no doubt it was her. On an impulse I got out of the car and went towards her.

"Hello," I said brightly. "Fancy seeing you here."

She turned and looked at me blankly for a moment and then said, "I wanted some peace and quiet."

"Oh, I'm sorry," I said hastily, and moved as if to go away. Then I stopped and said, "Esther, are you all right?"

Again the blank stare, and then, "I can't sleep. They've given me some tablets but they don't work. Or if I do sleep I have bad dreams."

"What sort of bad dreams?" I asked.

"About her."

"Her?"

"Jo. I can't get it out of my head."

"What is it?"

"Jo and Gordon. Just before he died . . ." Her voice trailed away.

"Surely not," I said.

"Oh yes, it's true. I followed him—to the stables."

"He did occasionally go up there," I said, "something to do with his friend Dan Webster's horse."

"Not the stables, her house. Several times."

"I'm sure there was a perfectly simple explanation."

She gave a bitter laugh. "Oh yes. She'd lost Charlie, so she wanted Gordon back."

"Look, Esther, I'm sure you've got it wrong. Jo wouldn't . . ."

"You don't know her like I do. She always wanted everything, even things I had that she didn't really want."

I shook my head. "I can't believe it," I said. "And, Gordon . . ."

"It wasn't his fault," Esther said quickly. "She had this hold over him, like she always did. Like she did in the old days. Just had to lift her little finger and he went running—every man did."

"Gordon married you," I said, "and you had two lovely children."

"And she took Simon away. All the time up at those stables, hardly ever at home, doing things for her. She was jealous because she didn't have any children, so she took Simon. Not Vicky though. Vicky saw through her," she said. "She knew what Jo was up to; she wasn't taken in."

Her voice rose sharply and a man walking his dog turned and looked at us curiously. I was worried about her. She was obviously in a bad state and I wondered how I was going to get her home.

"Gordon, poor Gordon," she went on. "He didn't know what he was doing." She looked at me pleadingly. "He did love me; he really did. But it was the same, just like it used to be; he couldn't help himself. Only *then* she went away. She wasn't going anywhere this time."

"Esther," I said, coaxing her, "don't you think you ought to go home? It's getting cold. There's quite a wind now."

She ignored me and stood looking out at the dull gray water. Then she said, quietly, almost resignedly, "I hated her. I've always hated her. I'm really glad she's dead."

Chapter Eighteen

For a moment I was silent. There didn't seem anything I could say.

"I was always second best," she went on in that same, quiet tone, "for Gordon and for Simon. I was used to that, I suppose, but then, after all those years, when I thought I was safe, she took him back. She won—just like she always did."

"No, really Esther," I said, "I'm sure you've got it wrong. Gordon may have gone to see Jo, but I think it was something to do with some land he wanted her to sell."

She ignored me; it was as if I hadn't spoken. "She could always make people do what she wanted. Everyone was fooled by that manner of hers, but I knew...."

Realizing that it was useless to argue with her, I concentrated on trying to get her home.

"Is your car here, or did you walk?" I asked.

That mundane question seemed to rouse her a little and she said, "I think I walked—yes, I wanted to get out of the house, to get some fresh air."

"Well, look, my car's just over there. Let me drive you home. I think it might be going to rain.

The wind's getting up too. Look, the sea's quite choppy."

Talking at random I managed to lead her over to the car and got her in. As we drove back she was silent and seemed quite passive. At the house I helped her take off her coat and persuaded her to stay in the sitting room while I went out to the kitchen to put the kettle on. While I was waiting for it to boil, I rang Simon on my mobile.

"Can you possibly get away and come home? Your mother's not well—I found her down by the harbor—she's very upset. I've got her home, but I don't like to leave her alone."

I made the tea and went back to find that Esther was sitting just as I'd left her. She drank her tea like an obedient child and we sat in silence for a while until, to my great relief, I heard Simon arrive. I went out into the hall and drew him to one side.

"I think she's having some kind of a breakdown. She was saying all sorts of wild things about your father and Jo. Really agitated. She's quiet now, but I didn't know what to do. Perhaps she should see a doctor?"

He nodded. "Yes, I think it's come to that. She's been like this several times since Father died and I did hope she'd get over it as time went on. Perhaps she should have professional help. But I can cope for the moment. Anyway, thank you, Sheila. I'm really grateful for all you've done."

We went into the sitting room and I said brightly, "Well, I'll be off now. Simon's here. I expect he'd like a cup of tea too."

She turned her head and gave me a vague smile. "It was nice to see you, Sheila. Do call in again when you're passing."

When I got home I felt I needed something stronger than tea, so I had a glass of sherry before making myself some lunch. I was still attempting to think through what Esther had said, but the animals chose to be difficult, wanting to be let out and then, almost immediately, in again, demanding extra food and attention, and making it impossible for me to concentrate on anything. I was just, finally, sitting down with a ham sandwich when the telephone rang. It was Simon.

"I thought I'd just let you know that I've got her to go and lie down for a bit," he said. "She wouldn't have any lunch, but I thought that if she managed to have a little sleep, she might be more herself when she woke up."

"She said she hadn't been sleeping," I said. "Perhaps that's part of the trouble."

"Dr. Macdonald prescribed some sleeping tablets, but she said they made things worse and stopped taking them."

"She told me they gave her nightmares," I said. "About Jo."

He sighed. "Oh dear, it's so difficult. She has this stupid idea, about Jo and Father. There's nothing in it, of course," he added hastily.

"No, of course not," I agreed, "but it seems like an obsession with her."

"Yes. And you're right. She does need some sort of professional help. That is, if she'll take it.

Anyway, I'll ask Dr. Macdonald what he thinks. He'll know whom to consult."

"That's the best thing. You've got enough on your shoulders just now. Can't Vicky help?"

"Well, you know how difficult it is for her, being a freelance and so forth."

"I don't see why you should bear all the burden yourself," I said sharply.

"I'll have to consult her anyway," he said, "before I make any arrangements for Mother. But I wanted to thank you again for looking after her. She hasn't gone wandering like that before. I'll somehow have to try to keep an eye on her."

"If there's anything I can do," I said, "you only have to ask."

"Bless you, Sheila. I'm so grateful." He paused. "I'd rather people didn't know. . . ."

"Of course not," I said. "I quite understand."

The thing that was uppermost in my mind, as I finally got to eat my sandwich, was the fact that Esther had followed Gordon. It seemed to show the sort of initiative—if that's what you could call it—that I hadn't expected of her. And if she'd always been resentful of Jo and the fact that Gordon had taken her as second best and had lived with that all these years, what, I wondered, had suddenly brought her to the point of this kind of obsessive jealousy? What had sparked it off? The fact of Charlie's death perhaps left Jo available again; but was that enough?

Tris's bark and a ring at the door interrupted these thoughts. It was Rosemary.

"Sorry to drop in, but Delia's got an hour's ride and it didn't seem worth going all the way home and then coming back again, so I thought I'd come and beg a cup of tea from you." She looked at me critically. "Are you all right? You look sort of confused and woolly. Is anything the matter?"

Rosemary and I always tell each other everything, and, anyway, Rosemary is Esther's friend too, so, as we went into the kitchen, I told her what had happened.

"Oh, poor Esther. It sounds as if she's really breaking up."

"She was fairly odd and emotional when I went to see her just before Gordon's funeral," I said. "But this is much worse."

"And all that stuff about Jo," Rosemary said. "She must have been brooding about it for years."

"I know. That's what's puzzled me. What made her suddenly do something as bizarre as following Gordon?"

"Well, perhaps she overheard part of a phone call—something like that—and got the wrong idea. I mean, any sort of connection between Jo and Gordon would have been enough."

"That's true," I said, pouring the tea. "Poor Esther, always trying to compete with Jo and knowing how impossible it was. I suppose that's why she made herself a sort of slave to Gordon. Whatever he wanted always came first; everything he did was always perfect. Remember how she used to go on about him?"

"Dreadfully sad, really. But really awful now. I

think I prefer Esther being irritating rather than Esther being pathetic."

"I suppose Gordon was trying to bully Jo into selling that land. That would be why he went up to the house rather than seeing her at the stables. Well, I'm sure he—and Dan Webster—got nothing out of Jo. I did try to tell Esther about it, but she didn't want to hear; she was so obsessed with her own theory."

"I do hope Simon can get some sort of help for her," Rosemary said. "It must be such a worry for him."

"He said he'd have to consult Vicky first. I do hope she doesn't cause any difficulties. After all, she's not around; Simon will have to cope with it all."

"Some sort of psychiatric help, I suppose," Rosemary said thoughtfully. "Vicky would have to agree."

"Do you think actually psychiatric?" I asked.

"Or possibly counseling—whatever that means nowadays. But she is obviously getting worse."

"Do you think," I said slowly, "with all that hate she had for Jo, she might have tried to do something to—well, to harm her?"

"You mean," Rosemary said bluntly, "did she kill her?"

"Well, yes."

"Are you still thinking it wasn't an accident?"

"You must admit it's a possibility."

"But Esther! Totally out of character!"

"Well, she did creep about following Gordon. You must admit that was out of character too."

"Yes, but . . ."

"And, after Gordon died, when she was in that funny sort of mood, she could easily have found some excuse for going up there, and you know how that office is left empty half the time with people out taking lessons or rides."

"It still doesn't sound like Esther to me."

"And," I said, "she didn't go to Jo's funeral."

"Well, nor did you," Rosemary said, "and you didn't kill Jo. She was ill like you."

"She could have pretended to be ill; it wouldn't have been difficult. Simon, and even Vicky, knew she'd been acting a bit strangely. They'd have been quite glad she didn't go."

"No really," Rosemary said, "I know you always like to find mysteries in everything, but I honestly don't believe that Esther killed Jo—or that anyone did for that matter."

"Oh well, perhaps you're right," I said reluctantly.

Rosemary looked at her watch. "I'd better get going. Though Delia wouldn't care if I never turned up."

"Do you mind if I come with you?" I asked. "I'd rather like to have an excuse for seeing how things are at the stables. You can drop me off at the end of the lane on your way back."

As we were approaching the stables I saw a familiar Mitsubishi driving away.

"That's Dan Webster," I said, craning my neck to make sure who the driver was. "I suppose he's been up here to persecute Simon again about selling those fields."

"Simon's no more likely to sell than Jo was," Rosemary said confidently.

Delia wasn't back yet, so I followed Rosemary into the office when she went to pay for the ride. Simon was sitting at the desk, studying some papers. He looked up when we went in.

"Hello, Sheila," he said, looking surprised at seeing me and obviously feeling that some explanation was needed for his presence at the stables during office hours. "I thought I might as well come up here; it was a bit late to go back to the office. But I got Mother settled all right before I left."

"That's good," I said.

"Simon," Rosemary broke in, "was Dan Webster up here trying to make you sell him those fields?"

"Dan Webster?" he said, rather taken aback by her tone. "Well, yes, as a matter of fact he was."

"And you're not selling?"

"No. No, of course not. I've told him so."

"He was round at the Butlers'," I said, "bullying them. But they're standing firm."

"Yes, I know," Simon said. "Will came here yesterday to tell me all about it. He was offering them fantastic prices."

"And he'd make fantastic profits," I said, "if he could get hold of this land for development now that there's this change-of-use thing from the council."

"He'd need planning permission," he said.

"Well, I don't think *that* would be a problem for Dan Webster," I said. "He's bound to have a councilor or two in his pocket—he's that sort of man." I stopped suddenly. "I'm sorry, Simon," I said. "I'd forgotten he was a sort of business partner of your father."

Simon smiled ruefully. "I'm quite aware of the sort of dealings my father was involved in," he said, "and I know what the general opinion of him was."

"Well, anyway," Rosemary said impatiently, "as long as neither you nor Will Butler will sell, the Webster man will have to look elsewhere for his nasty little schemes."

"I think it was really noble of the Butlers to hold out," I said. "They're terribly stretched financially and the sort of money he must have offered would have been a lifesaver for them. Thank goodness there are still people like them."

"And Simon, too," Rosemary said, smiling at him. "A hefty cash injection would have been very useful here at the stables. But you held out."

"Well," he said, shuffling the papers on his desk together and putting them away in a drawer, "even if I'd been tempted, I couldn't let Jo down. She'd never have sold."

"Well done, Simon," Rosemary said. "And speaking of money, here's what I owe you for Delia's ride. We'd better go and see if she's back yet."

When we got outside, the riders were back, but there was no sign of Delia.

"She's probably in the yard helping Liz and Peggy," Rosemary said. "I'd better go and root her out."

"Just before you go," I said, "what did you think of Simon, just now?"

"Simon? What do you mean?"

"Didn't you think he looked a bit uneasy?"

"Well, he looked tired, poor boy, but he's had quite a day, what with his mother going walk-about and then Dan Webster. . . ."

"Yes, I know, but did you think he sounded quite *sure* about Webster? I'm sure he's not thinking of selling," I said hastily, as I could see Rosemary rushing to the defense of her favorite, "but I got the impression that there was something about the affair he wasn't telling us. Something about his father, perhaps."

"That wouldn't surprise me."

"Well, you know, it's always been possible that since Gordon knew about this change of use long before it was made public, he could easily have told Webster about it so that they could make a nice little deal together."

"Probably."

"And, of course, that's what Gordon was going to see Jo about when Esther followed him."

"That's the thing that really gets me!" Rosemary said. "Esther of all people! How do you think she did it without Gordon knowing? I mean, she's not exactly my idea of a private eye."

"Well, I suppose he'd have said he was going to a council meeting and she'd have been suspicious, and when he drove off she got in her car and followed him. If he didn't go in the direction of the council offices but turned the other way, she'd know he was going to Jo's, so she could follow at a distance, if you see what I mean."

"I suppose so," Rosemary said grudgingly. "But it all sounds too clever for Esther!"

"I daresay when you're as jealous and obsessed as she was, you can do anything, however out of character it might seem. Anyway, after Gordon died, then Webster took over and tried to persuade Jo to sell, and when *she* died, Webster probably thought Simon would be easier to persuade. In fact . . ."

"No, Sheila. Not back to *your* obsession. Jo's death was an accident, whether it was more convenient for Dan Webster or not."

"Possibly."

I would have argued the point more fully, but Delia suddenly emerged from the stable yard and Rosemary seized the opportunity to hustle her into the car, where she held forth from the backseat.

"Gran, do you know, Peggy says I should be able to enter next year's Golden Horseshoes competition. I'll be old enough then. Only the ten-mile ride—or perhaps the fifteen if the going's good. So, will you sponsor me? Most people give a pound a mile. And would you sponsor me too, Mrs. Malory? And you could bring Alice to one of the checkpoints to see me. I'm sure she'd like that. It's very exciting. Of course, she won't be able to do it for years, but it would be good for her to see how it's done. This year, of course, it poured with rain and they had to cancel part of the course. Only a few people managed the thirty-five-mile course, but they were mostly sponsored by professional firms and things, which isn't really fair, is it?"

I escaped from this flow of information as Rosemary dropped me off at the end of my lane. As I walked back to the house I tried to remember what had made me think that Simon had been holding something back from us. There was nothing I could put my finger on, just the feeling that he was uneasy talking about it, a vague thought that there was something else. . . . I opened the front door and in the general coming and going, in and out, of the animals I lost track of the thought, whatever it was.

Chapter Nineteen

I'd fallen into a sort of postlunch doze, something that seems to happen to me more and more, when I was woken by the insistent ringing of the phone. I picked it up and heard Anthea's agitated voice.

"It's dreadful news," she said, "absolutely dreadful!"

"What is?" I asked, still only half awake and not yet capable of taking in any news, however dreadful.

"The lottery grant," Anthea said impatiently. "They've turned us down!"

"I'm sorry," I said inadequately.

"After all our hard work on the application—and Derek had lined up two independent referees as well for the next stage—it's really heartbreaking."

"How awful. Did they say why they've refused?"

"Oh, some bureaucratic nonsense—I couldn't be bothered with it. Of course," she went on, lowering her voice, "it's because we're not an inner city, not *deprived*. I know how these things work."

"Oh, I'm sure it's nothing like that," I said.

"Anyway," Anthea went on, "we're not giving up."

"But if . . ."

"We'll raise the money ourselves. After all, it's very necessary." She went into her usual getting-things-done mode and I listened with only half an ear. "Vital work . . . Health and Safety regulations . . . all pull together . . . committee meeting . . ." I came to abruptly when I heard her say sharply, "Well, Sheila, *can* you manage next Friday?"

"Oh," I said hastily, "I'm not sure. I'll look it up on the calendar and let you know."

"Very well," she said grudgingly. "And do you agree?"

"Agree?"

"About my idea for a sponsored walk. People raise thousands for them!"

"Well, yes, but for important things like cancer research, not for rewiring an old building."

"I can't imagine why you think making the wiring safe isn't important," Anthea said severely. "I'd have thought that considering what happened to poor Jo Hamilton—after all, she was a friend of yours—you'd be as anxious as I am to get it done!"

"Of course I am, but . . ."

"And all the committee will take part. We must set an example."

"I don't know how long the walk's going to be," I said, "but I'm afraid my knee can't manage more than a couple of hundred yards nowadays."

She made an exclamation of annoyance. "Oh well, you'll have to be a steward then; they stand about at intervals round the course with bottles of water, timing people. We'll arrange all that next Friday. The important thing is to get things moving."

"Yes . . ."

"I'm glad we've sorted things out. I'll get onto Maureen now and tell her that you agree with me that the sponsored walk is the best way to go. I'll get back to you when I know what she thinks. Good-bye."

"For heaven's sake—a sponsored *walk*!" I said as I put down the phone. Tris, who'd been lying peacefully in front of the electric fire, heard the last word and raised his head, looking hopeful, and then collapsed back again as I sat down on the sofa. Foss, now occupying my armchair, opened one eye, curled his tail round his nose and went back to sleep. I was thoroughly irritated by Anthea, and finding that my after-lunch coffee was now stone cold was the last straw. I slumped back on the sofa, knowing there were a thousand things I ought to be doing in the house and garden, but not feeling like doing any of them.

The phone's ringing again increased my irritation. For a moment I let it ring, sure it was Anthea getting back to me, but habit is strong and I've never been able *not* to answer the phone when it rings. I picked it up and said a cross "Hello." But it wasn't Anthea; it was Rosemary and she sounded upset.

"Oh, Sheila, I'm so glad you're in. I need to

speak to you, but not on the phone. Could you come round?"

"Now?"

"Please."

"What is it?"

"I'll tell you when you come."

She rang off and I replaced my receiver slowly, wondering what on earth it was all about. As I drove round there, I considered the various possibilities from something awful happening to one of the family (God forbid) to Mrs. Dudley being more intransigent than usual. By the time I got there I was really worried.

"What on earth's happened?" I demanded as Rosemary opened the door. "Is it one of the children?"

"No, nothing like that, but I didn't want to talk about it over the phone. Come on in and I'll put the kettle on."

Reassured by this, I followed Rosemary into the kitchen and sat down at the table while she filled the kettle.

"So, what on earth is it?"

"It's Simon."

"Simon? What's happened?"

"Well, you know Martin Krieger—Jack plays golf with him."

"I've met him once or twice. Some sort of high-powered businessman."

"That's the one. I don't know exactly what his business is, something to do with exports, but anyway, whatever it is, he has to entertain a lot of his overseas customers. What they mostly like to do is go to that rather plushy casino in Taunton."

"So?"

"So he's seen Simon there a couple of times."

"It can't be. He must have made a mistake."

"No, he knows Simon quite well—Simon's firm does his audit." Rosemary poured a cup of tea and pushed a plate of biscuits towards me. "The thing is," she went on, "he said Simon was on his own each time and was—what was the phrase he used?—'worryingly absorbed in the play.' So much so that he didn't see Martin. After the first time Martin kept an eye on him and saw that, though he did win occasionally, he went on gambling until everything was gone."

"How awful. When was this?"

"A while ago, before Jo died."

"So do you think it's serious?"

"Well, you know how fond Jack is of Simon—we both are—so he asked him to lunch and had it out with him."

"What did Simon say? Did he admit it?"

"At first he said he's only been once or twice, just to see what it was like. But after Jack pressed him, he more or less broke down and came out with the whole story. Apparently it started by chance when he logged on to some sort of poker thing on the Internet."

"I've heard about that," I said. "There was quite a bit about it in the papers a few weeks ago."

"That was just the beginning. He got really hooked, playing this wretched thing every night."

"Goodness, yes. I remember Esther saying he was up till all hours on his computer, but she thought it was work he'd brought home."

"Anyway," Rosemary said, "he started to go to this casino in Taunton, and casinos in London too when he went up to stay with Vicky."

"*Not* just wandering around London looking at things!" I said.

"Exactly."

"But the money?"

"Well, of course, he was dreadfully in debt—both credit cards to the limit and a loan from one of those companies—you know the ones that advertise."

"*Stupid* boy! So what did he do?"

"Apparently Jo came to his rescue. She lent him—gave really—enough to clear his debts on the understanding that he'd go to this Gamblers Anonymous place, and he said he would."

"And has he?"

"He says he has." She poured us both another cup of tea. "But Jack says he's not sure Simon's really given up gambling. He said he felt Simon was evasive—nothing you could put your finger on, but . . ."

"I know. That's what I felt when we asked him about Dan Webster—you remember—just a sort of *feeling*."

"Yes, you said. But we really don't know what to do now. Jack says we can't go on persecuting the boy about it; otherwise he'll never tell us anything.

But we can't just stand by and let him make a real mess of his life."

"It was really splendid of Jo," I said, "to bail him out like that. Especially when money was pretty tight."

"She had something of her own, and"—Rosemary hesitated for a moment—"and she gave him the money from Charlie's life insurance."

"Good heavens!"

"I know."

"That's quite something!"

"Well, that's what you do for your child," Rosemary said, "and Simon was the nearest thing she had to a child of her own. But I expect it's made the situation at the stables even more difficult."

"And that's another reason why Simon's got to pull himself together and make a go of things there. He owes that to Jo."

"That's what Jack told him."

"But of course," I said slowly, "if he *hasn't* given up and is in debt again, then perhaps he might be considering Webster's offer."

"Oh don't! I keep thinking of that. He couldn't—could he?"

"I suppose it depends how deeply he's in debt. He might be really desperate and there's no one else to bail him out this time."

"What about the money Gordon left him and Vicky?"

"I don't know how easy it would be to break the

trust. And, anyway, it would probably take ages and it would depend whom he's in debt *to*."

"You mean it might be someone . . . ?"

"Well, you do hear such awful things when people get mixed up in gambling and I don't think it just happens in television plays!"

"Oh don't!"

"I can't think of any way we can find out if he's still gambling, can you?"

"Actually, I can. I'll ask him."

"But Jack said . . ."

"Yes, but it would be different if I asked, not so *formal*, if you see what I mean."

"True. Yes," I went on, warming to the idea, "I think Simon's a bit nervous of men—even Jack. Something to do with his father, I expect. But he would respond to you. Now that Jo's gone, you are the one he'd turn to."

"Right, then," Rosemary said with sudden resolution. "Delia's got a two-hour ride tomorrow. I'll tell Jilly I'll take her to the stables. Two hours— longer if Delia starts cleaning the tack—should be long enough to have a proper talk." She leaned back in her chair and sighed. "Oh dear, *what* a mess. Why can't people lead straightforward lives!"

"If he is in debt," I said, "what will you and Jack do about it?"

"I don't know. Help somehow, I suppose—a proper loan, perhaps. Jack will know. The important thing is to find out exactly what's happened."

When I got home I was quite exhausted. What

with one thing and another it had been a peculiar day. Above all there was the awful feeling I had when Rosemary told me about Simon's problem. It was a feeling that I must keep to myself because I could never even suggest to Rosemary the possibility that if Simon was in debt and desperate and Jo had no more money to give him . . . I couldn't even formulate the thought in my mind, but it nagged away all evening. It was impossible, I was sure, that whatever the circumstances, Simon would even contemplate—no, he could never. . . .

I didn't sleep very well that night and I was just finishing a very early breakfast when Rosemary rang.

"Sheila, look, I don't think I can do this thing with Simon on my own. Will you come with me?"

"Of course I will, but are you sure? Won't it stop him opening up to you if I'm there?"

"No. I don't think so. You're an old friend and you were a very good friend of Jo too. And if he *is* still gambling and he promises to give it up, then you'll be another witness."

"I suppose so."

"And," Rosemary said, "I want you there so that I don't give up too soon; so that I really push him!"

"Fair enough. What time?"

"Delia's ride is at two, so about quarter to?"

"I'll be ready."

But will I really be ready? I wondered, when she'd rung off. I had to prepare myself somehow. On an impulse I put Tris into the car and went down to the beach. Even in the summer Taviscombe beach is almost always empty and this morning there was only one other dog walker in the far distance. The tide was right out—it looked as if you could almost walk all the way to Wales across the channel—and it was pleasant to walk on the hard, ribbed sand. I took a deep breath and tried to face the unthinkable.

If Simon was really in debt—really *badly* in debt again—and there was no more money to come from Jo . . . Well, then, he must have known that she would have left him everything—not just the stables, but the chance of the money that Dan Webster would pay for the fields. She would certainly have told him about that. He'd have gone through Gordon's papers and would probably have found stuff on the council's decision about the change of use of those fields before they'd been made public. So he'd have known just how *much* money Webster would have been prepared to pay. If he was desperate, *really* desperate, could he have wished . . . ? She was no longer young; she was unhappy, grieving for Charlie. Would it have been so impossible to convince himself that she might want to die? He was in and out of the stables all the time; it would have been so easy for him to have tampered with the wiring. . . .

Tris was running, barking at a large seagull that regarded him with contempt as he flew slowly away. I faced the possibility that a person I knew and liked might have planned the death—no, put it brutally—the *murder* of someone he loved. Gambling, I suppose, is a form of madness; you're not yourself—how could you be?—and when you're not yourself, you might be capable of something you wouldn't ever contemplate when you were in your right mind. Yes, Simon might have killed Jo. I'd faced the thought. But I didn't see how I was ever going to present that thought to Rosemary.

The other dog walker was approaching. I recognized the dog, running on ahead, before I recognized the owner. It was Roger.

"Hello, Sheila. You're out early!"

"So are you."

"It's such a lovely morning, I couldn't resist."

"Yes, it is," I agreed, suddenly realizing that he was right and that it was one of those perfect autumn mornings that still hold the warmth and brightness of summer.

Roger looked at me curiously. "Are you all right?" he asked. "You look a bit worried."

"No," I said hastily. Roger was the last person I could share my suspicions with. "I was just brooding about Anthea's latest idea—for a sponsored walk."

"Good God! Well, no one's going to persuade me to do more than put up the money for someone else to do it!"

"You'd better avoid Anthea then. You're just the sort of person she's looking for."

"I'll willingly sacrifice Delia and Alex," he said, "even Jilly!"

Tris had come running back to me. Roger's terrier, though perfectly amiable, played more energetically than Tris could manage. I bent to put his lead on.

"I'd better take this one home," I said. "He looks worn out!"

"Nice to see you," Roger said as he moved off. "I'll remember what you said about Anthea!"

What would Roger say, I wondered, if he knew what I'd been thinking? He'd laugh, I suppose, and wouldn't take it seriously. Jo's death was an accident—everyone said so; the coroner said so. I should put the thought out of my mind. Or, at least, see what Simon had to say this afternoon.

Chapter Twenty

Rosemary and I were both a bit on edge when she called for me the next day and were, I think, glad of Delia's flow of chat to cover up our silences.

"Emily's got this awful allergy thing—she comes out in ghastly blotches—and they thought she might be allergic to some horsey thing, so she was *dreadfully* upset, but it turned out to be a food allergy, so that was all right. Actually, there's a girl in my form who's gluten intolerant *and* lactose intolerant and when she goes out to tea she has to take her food with her in a sealed plastic box. . . ."

When we got to the stables and Delia had gone off on her ride, Rosemary looked at me and said, "Right. Let's do it." She knocked on the door of the office and we went in, closing the door behind us.

"Can I pay for Delia's ride now?" Rosemary said, putting some money down on the desk.

Simon looked up and smiled. "Hello," he said, "good to see you."

There was silence for a moment and then I said, "How's your mother?"

"Oh, good news. She seems much calmer now and a splendid thing has happened. Vicky's got to go to Montreal—some program she's doing about Canadian women writers—and Mother's going with her. Do you remember our cousin Phyllis? She and Mother were very close at one time, and then Phyllis married a Canadian and went out there. Anyway, he died last year and she's been on at Mother for ages to go out for a visit, so she agreed to go out with Vicky and stay for a while."

"That's marvelous," I said. "It'll do her the world of good."

We were silent again and Simon looked at us inquiringly.

"I'm sorry to go on about it, Simon," Rosemary said abruptly, "but we're really very worried about this gambling thing. Have you really given it up? Yes," she added, "Sheila knows all about it. You know she's fond of you too and is as worried as we are."

"I told you," Simon said, "I'm on top of it now."

"But there is something, isn't there?" I said tentatively. "I've felt it too—something that's really bothering you. Please, won't you tell us so that we can help?"

"No—really—there's nothing. . . ."

"That's nonsense and you know it." It was Rosemary at her most forceful. "Simon, we've known you all your life. It's perfectly obvious something is very wrong and it's tearing you to bits. If you really are coping with the gambling and it's something else, then *please* tell us. You know how much we care about you. You can tell us anything!"

Silence fell again as Simon sat motionless, not looking at us, staring down at the desk. Then quite suddenly he got up and went over to the small safe, opened it and took out a large brown envelope, which he put down in front of us.

"All right," he said very quietly, "perhaps you should know." He opened the envelope and took out a sheaf of foolscap pages covered with Jo's distinctive handwriting. "You were both her very good friends. I think she would like you to know how it was."

He laid the pages down on the desk.

"I'll leave you both to read it and then you'll understand."

He drew up another chair beside the one at the desk and went out of the office.

"What on earth . . . ," I began.

"Let's just read it," Rosemary said, and we sat side by side, reading together as we used to do sometimes when we were girls, sharing a favorite book. It was in the form of a letter.

Darling Simon:

I know you'll be shocked and saddened by the fact of my death and the way I died, but I must explain it all to you so that you'll see it was the best way. When I was young I had a foolish affair and couldn't cope with the pregnancy that finished it. I had an abortion, but, in those days, it was illegal and often done by unqualified people. Something went wrong and it left me not able to have children. I told Charlie about it before we were mar-

ried and he, bless him, was loving and supportive but, of course, there was a great gap in our lives. You, dear Simon, filled that gap for us and we'll always be grateful to you.

A while ago I began to suspect that I was developing Parkinson's. I didn't want to burden Charlie with the worry of it, so I went to see a specialist in Bristol and he confirmed it. It's been getting worse, but the symptoms weren't bad enough for me to tell Charlie before he died, so, thank God, he never knew. But I've always led such an active life and I couldn't bear the thought of becoming less active and, in the end, helpless, so I decided I didn't want to go on. I think you'll understand that and forgive me the sadness I know it will cause you.

You'll probably have guessed, though I never actually told you, that there's been a certain amount of pressure on me by Dan Webster and your father to sell our fields. Of course, I said it was impossible and I'd never do it. Unfortunately, some years ago when Charlie set up as a breeder—after his accident—he was going through a very bad time and desperately needed money to keep going. He was tempted, just the once, to do something illegal, something that affected the outcome of a race. He never did it again, and he gave up soon after and we moved down here. Anyway, somehow Gordon found out about it and threatened to make it public if I didn't sell the fields to him. Charlie was dead by then, of course, but I'd *do anything to protect his good name, and Gordon knew that.*

I knew if I refused outright, Gordon wouldn't hesitate to carry out his threat, so I tried to play for time. Years ago, before I went to London, Gordon asked me to marry him. Of course, I refused, but he's always had a sort of "thing" for me; I often used to worry that Esther knew about it and was unhappy. I took to inviting him up to the house in the evening, to have a drink, I said, and talk things through. I knew, as we all did, that his heart was bad and he was taking those beta-blocker things. Well, I read in the paper about someone who died after being given potassium while he was taking beta-blockers, and it gave me an idea. I'd got some potassium tablets; Charlie was given them to counteract the diuretic he was taking, and they were soluble and slightly fizzy and quite tasteless. So it was quite easy to put them in Gordon's gin and tonics when I made them for him.

So, yes, I killed your father and I am sorry because he was your father, though I know you and he never got on, but you do see how important it was for me to protect Charlie's good name, and Gordon was a sick man and he'd have died soon in any case. It's just that I needed him to die before I did.

You'll probably wonder why I chose such a strange way to die. I did it because I wanted it to look like an accident so that you'd get the insurance. I thought I might manage some sort of rid-

ing accident, but I realized that might damage the stables. Then one day I got a nasty shock from the electric kettle in the office when I was making the tea and that gave me the idea.

I've left a part share in the stables to Liz, as well as the house. If you've been a son to me, in recent years she's been the daughter I never had. Forgive a foolish woman, but I always hoped you two might make a go of it one day. If you ever do, remember you have my blessing!

I know I'm leaving the stables in good hands and I know you'll keep the promise you made me about the gambling. I trust you and I know you won't let me down.

You'd better keep this letter safe just in case there's any sort of complication. I'm sorry it's so disjointed and incoherent, but I've had to write it in bits as and when I could.

Darling Simon, I love you very much and I do hope you'll forgive the pain I've caused you. But I'm sure you'll understand why I couldn't go on. It's not just the Parkinson's, but doing without Charlie is too much for me to bear. What is it that hymn says? ". . . One step enough for me." You know why I have to do this.

All my love,
Jo

P.S. I think I'd like you to show this letter to Liz. I want her to know how it was.

When we had finished reading, we both had tears in our eyes.

"Poor Jo," I said.

"Poor Jo," Rosemary agreed, "and poor Simon too. What he must have gone through!"

The door opened and Simon came in. Rosemary held out her hands to him and he grasped them tightly.

"You poor boy," Rosemary said. "What a burden to place on your shoulders."

"She had no one else," Simon said quietly, "and she wanted me to know."

"And Liz," I said.

"Liz was wonderful when I showed her the letter," he said. "She's got me through. I couldn't have coped without her. And not just this"—he gestured towards the papers on the desk—"but the gambling thing as well. She drives me to the Gamblers Anonymous meetings, waits in the car and drives me back. She has faith in me. I know I mustn't let her down."

"That's wonderful," Rosemary said.

"Actually," Simon went on, "when Mother goes to Canada, I'm going to move in to the house here. Jo was right—we belong together."

"And Jo," Rosemary said, "what a sad, awful mess it all is. How can you deal with it? What can you do?"

Simon shook his head. "There's nothing I can do, except keep faith with her."

"But to take her life like that!"

"It was her choice," I said. "It would have been worse for her to go on."

"I suppose so," Rosemary said reluctantly. "But, Simon, what about your father? What about Gordon?"

"I've agonized about that," he said, "but what good would it do to tell anyone now? Jo's dead and just think what it would do to Mother. Father and Jo! It would tip her right over the edge, now, just when she seems to be getting back to normal."

"That's perfectly true," I said.

Simon gave me a grateful look. "Besides," he said, "we don't *know* those potassium tablets killed him. He was very ill anyway. And if those tablets were prescribed for Charlie, they might very well have been out of date."

"Yes," Rosemary said eagerly, "that's quite possible."

"That just leaves the insurance," I said.

Simon gave a short laugh. "Oh, that's not a problem," he said. "Apparently there was something in the small print in the policy about negligence and due care having to be taken and so forth. After the coroner said it was an accident waiting to happen, they were very reluctant to pay out."

"That wretched Marcus Barrington!" I exclaimed.

"And given the circumstances," Simon went on, "I didn't feel I could press them on that."

"Just as well," Rosemary said. "It might have

left you liable to all sorts of things if anyone found out about Jo."

"You won't say anything about any of this?" Simon said quickly. "Please."

"Well, I'll tell Jack, of course," Rosemary said. "I'm sure he'll be all right."

"And Sheila?" Simon looked at me anxiously.

"Of course not," I said.

"Thank you. For Jo's sake as well as mine."

We all sat there for a moment in silence. Then Simon said, "I can't begin to tell you how much it's helped me, telling you about it, showing you the letter—all that. I suppose it's sharing the burden, and explaining how things have been—well, it's helped me get things in perspective in a sort of way."

"You know we only want to help," Rosemary said.

"Actually," Simon said thoughtfully, "I think Jo would be pleased you knew. After all, you were among her oldest and best friends, and she would have been glad *I* had friends I could turn to. Liz is wonderful—she was marvelous about Jo and the letter and everything—but she's very young, and sometimes I worry about the age difference between us. And I know I'll be grateful to be able to talk occasionally about all this with—well, can I say older and wiser friends."

"Anytime, you know that," Rosemary said, getting to her feet. "Delia will be back from her ride. We'd better go."

"Anything we can do," I said, joining her at the door, "don't hesitate to ask."

Somehow being outside in the open air was an enormous relief. We went over and, leaning on the gate, looked out across the fields.

"Will Jack really be all right?" I asked.

"If I point out that the tablets had been prescribed for Charlie and were really *old*," Rosemary said, "then I'm sure he'll see that it was just wishful thinking on Jo's part."

"Anyway," I said, "Simon's right. It wouldn't do any good to show anyone else the letter and it would certainly do untold harm."

"I'm sure he'll keep it safe just in *case* there's ever a query—if anyone else was blamed, anything like that."

"Oh, I'm sure he will."

Rosemary sighed. "Simon's always been a bit weak. I suppose it's because he's always been frightened of his father and felt he was a disappointment to him."

"Well, now that he's got Liz," I said, "who looks up to him and thinks he's marvelous, I think he'll blossom, get some confidence at last. And I wouldn't be surprised if he only started this gambling thing because he was lonely and felt inadequate. That's something else that having Liz will help."

We silently considered this possibility.

"It's desperately sad about Jo," Rosemary said. "I can't imagine how she carried on as if everything were normal, when all that was going on!"

"Well, she was an actress," I said, "and a very good one. That was the last part she had to play."

"I never suspected the Parkinson's, did you?"

"No, not really, though now I know, looking back I suppose there were signs—the way she looked tired and strained sometimes, not riding so much. Come to think of it, that time I saw her in Bristol at Temple Mead station, she looked dreadful. I suppose she was on her way to see the specialist. No, she'd have hated being really ill, and I know how desperately she missed Charlie. I can see why she wanted to go."

We were silent again and as I looked down across the field, I had a moment of déjà vu. In the slanting rays of the late-afternoon sun I saw a tall figure on a superb horse coming towards us. But, as the figure grew nearer, I saw that it was Liz on Tarquin. We opened the gate for her; she dismounted and thanked us, smiled and led the horse into the stable yard.

"She looks so happy," I said.

"Life goes on," Rosemary said.

"Yes, life goes on," I agreed. "Thank goodness."